TUNNEL SECRETS

ROBERT W. SCHRADER

Jerry Burkley

Stories

BURKLEY BOOKS

Tunnel Secrets
All Rights Reserved
Copyright © 2019 Robert W. Schrader

Burkley Books
http://www.robertwschraderauthor.com

Paperback ISBN:978-1-7331203-0-2 [KDP   Publishing]
E-Book   ISBN: 978-1-7331203-1-9 [KDP Publishing]
Hardback ISBN: 978-1-7331203-2-6 [PENDING]

Cover Image by Betty A. Schrader

PRINTED IN THE UNITED STATES

DISCLAIMER

This is my book. TUNNEL SECRETS is the second novel in the Sheriff Jerry Burkley Stories series. This is my own alternate universe. I have used, with permission, names of real people and some actual events. I have changed them to reflect my story and not the actual event. I took great joy in creating more of my universe. My memories and remembrances of many years ago may have converted it all into fiction anyway! I have not tried to portray any of my characters as having done what they did (unless, of course, they did.)

Bob Schrader

ACKNOWLEDGMENTS

Friends allowed me to use their name and sometimes capture part of their personality in Jerry's Story. Those who didn't get killed off (only one) are in Tunnel Secrets. Read about them in Jerry's Story. Each of them is a vital part of the storyline, and I am appreciative of being allowed to continue having them participate. I have found it fun to visualize my character, even if it doesn't resemble that person in the book. You all live in my alternate universe. Thanks for being there.

In *Jerry's Story*, William (Bill) H. Jones was portrayed as an attack helicopter pilot who volunteered to fly medical "Dustoff" missions when he was needed. On his last flight, Bill's helicopter was hit by an rpg (rocket propelled grenade). He was killed in action. President John R. Burks (another name on loan) presented the Medal of Honor to Bill's wife, Kathleen.

Bill was hard to 'kill off'. Willy J. is a contractor in real life but was never a deputy sheriff. Bill Jones is one of my neighbors in Casa Grande, Arizona. In *Tunnel Secrets* Bill becomes Willie J, the iconic contractor, and the go to guy. Bill's name went to our intrepid K-9.

Willy J is a reserve deputy with the Banner County Sheriff's Department. Kathleen continues to hang out with us.

The sheriff's department gains two dogs. One is a retired service dog, and the other is a K-9 patrol dog. Taking on two new dogs in *Tunnel Secrets* meant I needed a K-9 officer/dog trainer. I had to find a dog too. Fortunately, I know a great dog trainer. Louis Robinson is the real thing. Louis is a former Air Force K-9 handler and trains dogs for a living. He is my service dog's trainer. And a great one.

I also know a great dog breeder.Lisa Sloan is also the real thing. She breeds the best Labrador retrievers in the world. She gave me my service dog almost four years ago. I asked Lisa if she would be willing to donate another dog to a law enforcement agency (long pause), in my next book. She immediately said, "yes." Lisa is another 'type cast' person. Lisa frequently donates one puppy out of each litter to a disabled veteran. Thanks, Lisa for all you do for Vets!

Thanks to Lisa and Louis, I have Dusty.

Some of the things I attribute in the book are fiction. In my alternate universe, Louis moves his training operation, Robinson Dog Training, to Caribou, Wyoming.

Tom McCall is a fabulous teller of tales. Tom is another neighbor in Casa Grande. Tom 'Cash' McCall owned an automobile dealership in Canada for many years. He gave me input and quickly agreed to be part of *Tunnel Secrets*. Tom in the book is Tom in real life. Rarely does Tom remove his hat; he doesn't take it off in the book, but once.

Chuck was in *Jerry's Story*. I mention him again to apologize. I confused his retired Air Force rank and the Army rank structure I used in the book. I demoted him one grade. Chuck allowed as how that was ok since I promoted him in the book. Thanks for all you do Chief.

Tunnel Secrets features a brave young girl facing death, an unknown future, and many challenges, with the charm and curiosity of a cat. Brynna (with two n's) is my granddaughter. Brynna asked me if I would put her in my next book. How could I say NO!

Brynna poised some challenges. Brynna's mother was in *Jerry's Story* as Chris Roads (C-40). I had already begun *Tunnel Secrets*. Brynna wanted to be Chris's Daughter in *Tunnel Secrets*. Since I don't know where I am going with a book until I write it (even if I think I do), Brynna became an orphan and a key figure in solving several major criminal investigations. Thanks, Brynna (with two n's). (An inside joke. One of our best friends used to kid Brynna about only having only one n and she always responded "it is Brynna with two n's"). Thanks, Bear!

And THANKS to all those who have read my books, and especially those who wrote reviews. Reviews helped *Jerry's Story* get a national award. (American Fiction Awards Finalist for Best New Fiction). It made my day!

Special thanks to my aunt, Mildred Hunter. Aunt Mildred call me often to visit. Aunt Mildred keep asking me about the tunnel from the funeral home under the building where I grew up, to the Wyoming capitol building. (There isn't one!) Her questions about a tunnel gave me some good ideas. Now there is a tunnel. Thanks, Aunt Mildred.

Betty Schrader is in both books, but of greater importance is the support and help she has given me as I take on being an author in my old age. Betty encourages me, allows me to read excerpts to her, (sometimes), and gives me sage advice. Betty designed the covers for *Jerry's Story, Tunnel Secrets,* and for the next book about Sheriff Jerry Burkley, *Raven Kindness.*

THANK YOU ALL!!

BOB SCHRADER

TUNNEL SECRETS

TABLE OF CONTENTS

"THERE IS LIGHT AT THE END OF THE TUNNEL"

-popular idiom

TO BETTY WITH ALL MY
LOVE

TUNNEL SECRETS

by

ROBERT W. SCHRADER

DEAD BODY IN BANNER COUNTY

The dispatcher at the Banner County Sheriff's Department answered the call. "911, what is your emergency?" The phone line went dead. "Sergeant Carson," said Jenny Abbote, the night dispatcher. "I think we may have a problem!"

"What?"

"A hang-up!"

"So! We get a lot of those."

"True, but the caller advised it was a dead body with a gunshot wound!"

"Trace it back if you can, Sergeant Fred Carson used his department cell phone to call the sheriff.

"Hey, Boss, we may have a shot fired 911 call."

Sheriff Flannigan said, "more!"

"Nothing yet, but Jenny is trying to trace it."

"Ok, let me know, and thanks," said Big Tom.

Sheriff 'Big Tom' Flannigan was the Sheriff of Banner County, Wyoming. The county seat is in the town of Caribou, Wyoming, (population about 5,000 people). The whole county may have 40,000 people. The low population accounts for the number '33' used for the automobile license plate prefix. The county north of Banner County, Canyon County, (population 20,000) has a license prefix of '26'. Cheyenne, the capitol of Wyoming, in Laramie County (population 50,000), has a '2' designation.

Banner County is small, but a great place to live. There is virtually no crime. Probably due to Sheriff Flannigan and the Caribou Police Chief, Stands Tall Ferguson. Stand Tall's mother was Cheyenne Indian. His father was 'Old' Silas Ferguson. Ferguson owned and managed Ferguson Savings and Loan. Silas built a fortune making small loans to local farmers and ranchers. He was wealthy! Stands Tall is not rich. He is an honorable man and an extremely proficient police chief. Stands Tall and Tom work as a team to shield Banner County residents from danger. A dead body in Banner County motivates Stands Tall and Tom to high alert.

"911, what is your emergency?" Jenny was both ready and surprised at the caller's answer.

"I am hiking along Antler trailhead to Anthem Peak. My cell phone keeps going out."

"Did you call earlier?" asked Jenny.

"Yes, but the phone dropped out!"

"What can I do for you?"

"There is a dead body near the trail. I'm a nurse, so I know it's a dead body with a gunshot wound!"

Jenny advised, "please stay where you are. I will send a helicopter for you." The Banner County Sheriff's Department had just acquired a Bell Jet Ranger using federal grant money. The department had three deputies qualified and licensed as commercial pilots, assigned to fly aircraft for the Banner County Sheriff's Department. Jerry Burkley and Carlita Camino (aka Chris Roads) were licensed fixed-wing pilots. Chris and Jerry were the Cessna 206 pilots. Bob Schrader and Jerry were former Army helicopter pilots. Burkley and Schrader were authorized and qualified to operate the Jet Ranger. Schrader was the Chief of the Banner County Sheriff's Reserve department and worked as a volunteer. Chris was a full-time deputy but couldn't fly the Jet Ranger.

Jerry, who was a full-time deputy and shift supervisor, was the department's only helicopter pilot. Guess who got called? Jenny liked waking up the new lieutenant.

Jerry didn't like his sleep disturbed. "What do you want?" he growled into the phone.

"Want to fly?" asked Jenny

Jerry liked flying, fixed or rotary-wing, and his tone softened. "When, where, and why?" Burkley answered.

"There is a lady hiker near Anthem Peak. She found a dead body," Jenny explained.

'On the way." Jerry loved to fly. Jerry enjoyed being in law enforcement. He especially favored mixing both activities. As a lieutenant, Jerry had a personal patrol car; a new Pontiac with lights, siren, and radios installed. He quickly drove to Caribou Airfield. After opening the hangar doors, he pushed N3320SD, the Banner County Jet Ranger, onto the pad in front of the large hangar.

Lights swept across the pad area. Sheriff Tom Flannigan, who monitored all the radio traffic, drove in. "Hi, Sheriff," Jerry greeted him, "I didn't know this assignment was on the radio."

"It wasn't. Jenny thought you might need some help."

"I did before you got here! Sierra Delta is hard to push! You have great timing."

"Well, my intentions were good. Where are we going?"

Jerry knew he was going to have company. Sheriff Tom liked to fly almost as much as Jerry did, but as a passenger. On the other hand, having an experienced investigator along was beneficial. Four eyes were better than two, and Tom could help load the body. *Thank you, Jenny,"* thought Jerry to himself.

Jerry completed his pre-flight walk-around of the Jet Ranger, seated himself in the right seat (the aircraft commander's place). He fastened his lap and shoulder belts, while Sheriff Tom buckled into the left side seat. The checklist complete, Jerry yelled. "clear!", started the turbine engine, and carefully watched his engine instruments move into the green.

Sheriff Tom, although not a pilot, had been on many flights. Tom turned the radio to 122.8 MHz, (the unicom frequency used at airports without working control towers). The sheriff keyed the radio mike with a push switch on the control stick, and transmitted, "November Three-Three-Two-Zero-Sierra-Delta, light on the skids for takeoff on runwayTwo- Six."

"Hey, you're getting the radio work Sheriff."

"Thanks."

Jerry adjusted pitch and collective, made a 360-degree pivot to watch for other aircraft, and hovered. He then angled forward to gain airspeed and lifted into the night sky.

The rotatable spotlight mounted underneath the Jet Ranger illuminated a woman waving. She was wearing outdoor gear and a backpack. Jerry landed the helicopter softly on the ground in a clearing nearby.

"Howdy ma'am, my name is Flannigan. I'm Banner County Sheriff. The pilot of that contraption is Lieutenant Burkley. Did you call about a dead body?"

"Yes, I did. It's about a hundred yards that way," she said, pointing west.

Jerry shut down the helicopter. He and the sheriff walked to the body.

"Not good, Sheriff. That's a gunshot wound in the head."

"Better call for a forensic team and the coroner."

"Yup," said Jerry, as he turned and walked back to 20SD. Jerry knew his portable radio wouldn't be practical. The one in the Jet Ranger had more power and range.

THE AMERICAN LEARNS ABOUT TUNNELS

The American was pleased with himself. After only three weeks in a foreign country, he felt confident enough to travel alone, order meals, and pass unnoticed. He sought housing in a hotel in the Schwarzwald region of southern Germany. Months of language training had given him the ability to speak the German language. The last three months gave him the gestures, mannerisms, and customs of the people where he was living. Only last week, while skiing at Davos, Switzerland, about a three-hour drive from his hotel, he was able to pass himself off as German.

It was snowing when he returned to the Hotel Zur Sonne and let himself into the small hotel room. Flakes of snow fell in gentle puffs as he looked from the window to survey the scene before him. Soon it would be too late to turn back!

The bar and restaurant at the Hotel Zur Sonne in Donaueschingen, Germany, was cozy and relaxing. The American, Wesley Winegar, locked the door to his room. Winegar walked down the narrow stairway and entered the bar area. Wesley seated himself at a table for four, where he could sit with his back to the wall. Winegar could observe both doors and everyone in the room from this location. He ordered 'Fürstenberg' draft beer. Getting the beer prepared for him was a lengthy process. The foam settled several times before the liquid was level with a mark engraved on the beer glass, with almost no foam. Then, and only then, did the proprietor bring Wesley his beer. Winegar was sipping his beverage when a stranger approached the table.

"Dr. Livingston, I presume," said the slight man before him. The man was wearing a Bavarian-style cap and an overcoat. He was carrying a large briefcase held shut with two wide straps.

"And you must be Henry Morgan Stanley!" This dialog and several other equally corny exchanges were the passwords and responses used to authenticate each other's identity.

Herr Rudolph Gulde was an Anwalt (lawyer) in a large legal firm in Stuttgart. His function in this transaction was to convey information to Wesley so sensitive it could not be mailed, or even put in written form. Thus, the need for two strangers to meet face-to-face.

Rudy Gulde told Wesley everything he knew about a tunnel leading to an underground vault. The vault contained possibly the most important, most vital, and most valuable object imaginable.

"Be very careful, my friend," warned Rudy. "If you move it, hide it well! Tell no one what I have told you."

"Thank you. Watch your back. You too are in danger!"

The two men parted and went their separate way. Wesley did not return to his room. He hiked cross-country, avoiding congested areas and shunning both public and private transportation. Several weeks later

Wesley boarded a commercial air flight from Amsterdam, Holland, to Toronto, Canada, using a different name and identification.

<<< >>>

"Banner County Sheriff's Department, Jerry Burkley speaking, what can I do for you?"

"Jerry, this is Hank Toshman."

"Good morning Doc, or should I call our new Banner County Coroner Doctor? You can call me Jerry. Welcome to Caribou."

"Either is fine. I answer to Hank, Dr. T, Doc, Doctor Toshman, or most any other friendly greeting. It's nice to be here, thanks."

"What can I do for you, Hank?" Jerry earnestly replied. Jerry already liked the guy.

"Your John Doe from Anthem Peak may or may not have died from a gunshot to the head."

Jerry was puzzled. He had seen the wound in the forehead. "The dead guy sure did look like he had been shot!"

"Oh, he was shot. The bullet was a .45 caliber most likely from a model 1911. I recovered the round, and it looks like a military issue slug. The problem is the autopsy suggests the cause of death was from being 'frozen'. It is August in Wyoming, and it has been hot!"

Jerry leaned forward in his desk chair and started making notes on his desk pad. "Strange. Any theories?"

"A couple; shot first and put in a freezer; put in a fridge and then shot. Maybe died on his own, iced and then shot. My problem is the autopsy results don't support any of my speculations. I'll keep looking, but I thought you should know."

"Thanks, Hank. I'll let Tom know. Maybe our investigators will find something to help fill in the blanks.

"Nice talking with you. Hope we can meet face-to-face sometime soon."

Jerry hung up the phone and went to find Sheriff Tom. Jerry was sure Big Tom would be interested in this development. The sheriff was very attentive. "Let me get this straight. We have an unknown person found dead in Banner County. No one knows how he died. We don't know who done it, or why. Is that about it?"

Jerry shook his head. "We don't know how he got to Anthem Peak either."

The sheriff shook his head. "Ok, send Carlita Roads to interview the lady who found the body, Ms. Nancy Carmichael. Have Casey (Sergeant Casey Brown) use some of his shift deputies to recheck the area to see if they can find any witnesses. Put in a request for information from NCIS (National Crime Information System, a computer system for law enforcement)".

"On it." Responded Jerry. "And Carlita is called Chris Roads."

"Ok, see if you can get the feebies (FBI) out of first gear. They should have been able to provide an identity by now," the sheriff growled, "and I know her name is Chris."

"My pleasure, Boss," chuckled Jerry, who was aware of the high regard and praise Tom had for federal agencies, particularly the mighty Federal Bureau of Investigation (FBI).

In this instance, the FBI was of some help. The feebies called Banner County. "Sheriff Flannigan, this is SAIC (Special Agent in Charge) Cheyenne, Zeke Flores."

<<< >>>

Jerry was tired! The investigation at Anthem Peak consumed the rest of the night and many daylight hours the next day. Travel to the peak forced those on scene to wait. Jerry, Chris, and Bob, moved responders by flying ferry flights for personnel and their equipment. Sheriff Tom was tired as well.

"Jerry, last flight. I think you are out of flying hours."

"Yes, Sir let's head home. Joe and Casey can handle the rest."

Jerry and Tom had been on the job for over fourteen hours with little sleep the night before.

"Jerry," called Lieutenant Joe Pawlik, "can I ride along? I have lab samples for DCI. Grant (Wyoming Highway patrolman Grant Baldwin) will meet me at Caribou Airfield and transport them to Cheyenne."

"Sure, climb on!"

Big Tom inquired, "you all done?"

"Nope! but Casey is doing well. I'm going to help Roads and Schrader conduct witness interviews."

"Forge ahead, Joe. Good hunting for connections."

"I shall. Sheriff, Edna called and said to go straight home," Joe chuckled. (Edna is Tom's wife. Many deputies think she is in charge!)

Caribou Airfield was a welcome stop for Tom and Jerry. Both went home tired, but content they had performed law enforcement to the best each could do. Joe went to find C-40 (Chris Roads) and C-20 (Bob Schrader).

Jerry slept late. His cell phone woke him mid-morning. After a quick look at the caller ID, he chirped, "hi Pretty Lady."

"Hi yourself. What would happen if it wasn't me calling?"

"Depends! First, I would worry about you. Then I would see what developed."

"Oh, you're terrible! Want to take me to lunch? We can talk about the new house."

"What new house?"

"Oh, that is even worse than your 'what develops' comment! The house we are buying and going to remodel."

"That one? Ok, we can talk. First, I better talk to Willy J and see what it's going to cost."

"That might be a good idea. Pick me up at twelve! I've got to go. Bye." Cheryl hung up.

Jerry's day began!

<<< >>>

Chris was pleased to have been selected to do an interview. *Maybe I will get to be a detective*, she wondered. *That would mean a promotion.* Thinking for a moment, Chris realized there weren't any detectives in the Banner County Sheriff's Department. Just a sheriff, undersheriff, and deputies! "Nuts," she said aloud, as she pulled the Palmer file out of the steel file cabinet.

Bob Schrader, Chief of the reserve deputies, with the rank of lieutenant within the Banner County Sheriff's Department. (Schrader was a retired Army colonel and had been chief of staff for Senator John Burks) said, "got a problem, Chris."

Bob liked being a deputy and spent a lot of time as a volunteer. He didn't get paid as a deputy, but he performed the same duties and assumed the same risk of not living through his shift, like all the other deputies. He and the other twelve reserve officers were highly respected!

"Just talking to myself."

"Must be a good audience! Are you my partner for interviews today?"

"Yes, Lieutenant. Sergeant Brown said to help you interview the nurse who found the body and anything else you need in the Palmer investigation. Deputy Roads was somewhat in awe of Bob Schrader.

"Do you have the file?"

"Yes, Sir! Nurse Carmichael works swing shift at Banner County Memorial, so she will probably be home now."

"If she isn't hiking, shopping, on a date, or something," Bob commented. "Let's go find out. Your car or mine?" Bob was aware new deputies loved their assigned patrol car and always wanted to drive.

No surprise when Chris said, "Let's use Charlie Forty." Charlie 40 was Chris's badge number. 'C-40' was emblazoned on the left rear of the trunk deck of her assigned car.

"Lieutenant, why does Banner County have reserve deputies? The department seems like we have a full staff. What are reserve deputies anyway?"

Bob grinned, leaned back in the passenger seat and observed, "just full of questions tonight, aren't you Rookie?"

"Only way to learn, Sir!"

"Fair enough. I'll try to teach you what I know."

"Please!"

"Well, we have reserve deputies because Jerry Burkley told Sheriff Tom some reserves might be helpful when Senator Burks calls."

Puzzled by his answer, Chris said, "I don't understand. Clarify!"

Bob complied with Chris's request. "Jerry, Rios, and I sometimes get a call from Senator Burks asking for our help. Hard to say no to him. We have all served with the senator forever. Senator Burks was an Army captain when we all met. He became a four-star general, retired from the Army, and ran for the United States Senate from Oklahoma. He still is the Oklahoma Senator. Jerry, Rios, and I, sometimes work projects for him. Reserves take our place when we are gone."

"What kind of projects?"

"Missions involving national security of some sort usually, and almost always classified so we can't talk about them, at least while they are ongoing."

Chris protested, "but you are a reserve deputy. Does that mean you have a *reserve*-reserve deputy?"

Bob laughed! "yup, Willy J takes over for me when I'm gone." Willy was a local contractor and a long-time reserve deputy. No one knows why William (Willy) Harold is called 'Willy J', but that's his nickname."

Chris drove the Charlie 40 car into Nancy Carmichael's driveway. Chris asked, "more later?"

"Promise," replied Bob. "Now, we need to get to work."

Chris knocked on the front door of a neat, well-maintained, ranch-style house. Bob tapped Chris on the arm and motioned for her to move to one side of the door as he stood. Not in front, but off to one side. Chris quickly complied and commented, "I thought she was a witness, not a perp (a criminal perpetrator)!"

15

"She is, but you need to learn habits that might save your life sometime. Do you know who's behind that door?" Bob asked quietly.

"No! Oh! yes, I get it."

Nancy Carmichael opened the door right then. "Hi, pilots. Come in. What can I do for you?"

Bob explained, "I'm Lieutenant Schrader, and this is Deputy Roads. Although we are pilots for the sheriff's department, we are both deputies. We have been assigned to interview you formally. Would that be all right, and is this a convenient time?"

"Of course, come in! Lieutenant, I think I've seen you at Banner County Memorial Hospital where I work?" It was a question.

"Yes, ma'am." I am the assistant hospital administrator.

"Is the pay so low you have to work two jobs?"

Bob grinned, "my only paid job is at the hospital. I'm retired Army. I volunteer to be a reserve deputy for Banner County. I am here in that capacity."

Nancy turned to Deputy Roads. "Do you work extra jobs too?"

"No, I'm just a deputy. That's plenty!"

All three chuckled. Nancy got everyone seated, and the formal interview got underway. Bob set up a recording machine, and asked Nancy for permission to use the device, identified those present, and gave the Banner County case number and name. He then looked at Chris and nodded.

"Ms. Carmichael, as you know, my name is Chris Roads. I am a sheriff's deputy, badge number Charlie Forty. I will be conducting the initial phase of this interview. The interview went smoothly. Occasionally, Bob asked a question to clarify Carmichael's answer, but rarely. Chris did a comprehensive and efficient interrogation.

Chris requested Nancy Carmichael to appear at the sheriff's office in Caribou, to read and sign a transcript of the tape, under oath, that it was a true and correct copy of her testimony.

Nancy said goodnight to the two law enforcement officers. Bob was picking up on reserve history when a vehicle with no lights (it was well after dark) drove onto the main road in front of Chris's patrol car. Chris said, "that's asinine! Maybe we have a DUI (driving under the influence or drunk driver)." Chris flicked switches to turn on the overhead red and blue flashing lights on the car's light bar. The unconventional driver in front continued; unconcerned, with no lights on, and drifting back and forth across the highway. Chris used the siren and ultimately used the high-power spotlight to shine a bright light in the driver's rear-view mirror. The driver pulled to the roadside. Chris and Bob approached the vehicle on foot. Just as Chris reached the driver's door, the automobile moved slowly away, weaving across the center lane. Bob and Chris hurried back to the patrol car and continued the chase.

Radio transmissions from Charlie 40 to sheriff's dispatch were heard by other field units and the two shift supervisors (Lieutenant Pawlik and Sergeant Brown). Even the Sheriff was listening. That night Chris learned the meaning of 'Silence is Golden'. The deputies, who had all incurred similar problems, snickered and some even roared with glee. A lieutenant and a rookie weren't being obeyed or respected. Ultimately the use of overhead lights, siren, and spotlight resulted in a full stop of the other automobile. At least until the older woman behind the wheel was asked to step out of the car so the deputies could conduct field sobriety tests. The inebriated woman politely complied. One minor problem ensued. As the older woman got out of the car, she took her foot off the brake pedal. The automobile moved slowly forward. Bob jumped into the car and pushed on the brake pedal. He got the vehicle stopped and put the gear shift into park. Bob was lying part-way across the front seat. The activity knocked Bob's hat off, and he was mildly upset.

"Lieutenant," said Chris, "she is a DUI. Can I cuff her, take her to the jail, and throw the key away." Chris's comment was a statement, not a question.

"Know how you feel Chris, but no, you can't. Might get heat for that!"

The two deputies eventually did take Mrs. Velma Cooksen to the jail. Mrs. Cooksen was seated in the back seat of Chris's car without handcuffs. Bob didn't think Mrs. Cooksen was a security risk. Vema Cooksen continued to be an irritant to Deputy Roads. The elderly lady sat with her back to the passenger side door and placed her legs across the back seat. Chris could see her in the rear-view mirror or by turning her head. Bob couldn't.

Mrs. Cooksen politely answered all the lieutenant's questions, which were intended to help get her home sometime soon. Every time Mrs. Cooksen responded to a question, the inebriated driver stuck her tongue out or made a funny face. Chris wanted to melt the jail key immediately after Mrs. Cooksen was locked up. Bob prevailed. Velma Cooksen went to her own home with her daughter. Mrs. Cooksen was probably tucked into bed before Deputy Roads completed writing her arrest report!

Deputies were in the briefing room when Bob and Chris came in. "Way to stop em," one deputy quipped.

 Bob quickly commented, "Wasn't it nice of Velma Cooksen to help me teach our rookie how to make DUI stops?" That question took away the tension and relaxed everyone.

A few days later, Chris felt much better about this episode. While speaking to the Justice of the Peace, Barney Coleson, Mrs. Cooksen commented, "this deputy," pointing to Forty, "was so nice to me, but he," gesturing to Lieutenant Schrader, "wasn't nice at all!"

Chris almost lost it in the courtroom. She wanted to roll on the floor, laughing. She didn't! Forty still works for the sheriff's department.

"Lieutenant, you didn't know me. Why did you recommend me to be a deputy?"

"Another story, another day. Back to work.

FILES AND STUPID PEOPLE

Carol Ray, the duly elected County and Prosecuting Attorney for Banner County, Wyoming, knocked on the door to Jerry Burkley's office.

"Morning, Carol," greeted Jerry. "Have a seat. What can I do for you this fine morning?"

Carol sat in one of the two comfortable chairs before Jerry's desk. I have a problem needing your, or maybe the sheriff's, assistance!"

"And that would be?"

"Judge Broderick asked, no ordered, TG (Tashana Gonzalo, the judge's court reporter) and me to find a location to store old court records and move the records to the new location."

"Nice of the Honorable James F. Broderick, our esteemed district court judge! How can the sheriff's department assist?"

Carol breathed a sigh of relief. The county and prosecuting attorney leaned back in her chair. "Two immediate problems. First, we must find a place for storage that will be dry, secure, and accessible. The second is easier. We need some help in moving boxes. Don't say use prisoners. The files are court records. Anyone with access has to be trusted."

"Ok, I have prisoners that are trustees, but I suppose they fit in the untrustworthy category as well," Jerry replied. "I understand the problems, I think. Let me call an expert, or at least someone that may have some good suggestions. Cheryl may kill me, though!"

"Who?" Carol was more curious than concerned but also asked, "why would Cheryl do you harm?"

"Because she wants the house at least livable!"

"What are you talking about?" Carol blurted.

"My expert is our house remodel contractor, Willy Harold. If this takes a lot of Willy J's time, he won't be working on the house Cheryl, and I just bought."

"I thought you had a place in Caribou."

"We do. It is a rental. We bought the Fox Run place, and the house needs lots of work," Jerry said, shaking his head.

Carol persisted, "why would it take a lot of time? We can't hire an expert. Judge Broderick didn't give us any money for the move. That's why Tashana and I decided to ask you for help."

"That's the good news." Jerry grinned and pointed to the chart of the Banner County Reserve Deputies hanging on the wall behind Carol. "Willy J is second in command of the reserves, knows all the property around Caribou, and is my house contractor. Cheryl will probably kill me!"

Carol, TG Gonzalo, and Willy J were soon intently engaged in discussions about a good location for records storage. Soon they had a short list of places to explore! This news made Jerry very happy. He might not get killed after all!

Cheryl didn't kill me! She was far to fascinated by the three historic buildings on the proposed storage area list. One was a landmark bar in downtown Caribou. Originally the building was a liquor warehouse. Legend or rumors suggested tunnels led to houses of 'ill repute' which were utilized by local businessmen for mid-day appointments. Willy J advised TG and Carol, "the ground and upper floors would both meet your storage requirements."

"What about tunnels? Are there any?" asked Cheryl.

"We didn't find any," Willy answered. "But we weren't planning to store records in the basement, so we didn't search that thoroughly."

Jerry wanted to get on with his house remodeling but was concerned about the prospect of undiscovered tunnels.

"How would the tunnels affect record security?"

"Hadn't considered that, Boss," Willy conceded. "I'll take another look."

Jerry didn't look happy. TG and Carol both grinned but didn't laugh at Jerry's expression.

Jerry's and Willy J's portable radios crackled to life. "Charlie Two, Robert Two (Jerry and Willy's call signs), rtb – asap!" (return to base as soon as possible).

Jerry keyed the microphone hooked to his shirt and answered, "Charlie Two, Robert Two, copy."

The records team, as they had begun to call themselves, assembled in Jerry's office. Sheriff Tom entered and commanded, "everyone to the briefing room!"

When the team entered the sheriff's briefing room, they discovered the entire Banner County Sheriff's Department were present, except a group of reserve deputies on patrol,

"What's happening Sheriff?" Jerry queried.

"Re-alignment announcement," answered Sheriff Flannigan.

Tashana, thinking like a court reporter who chronicled legal events, asked, "who is getting fired?" TG assumed re-alignment meant someone was going to be terminated.

Sheriff Tom answered TG's inquiry as he addressed the assembled deputies and staff. "This department has four shift lieutenants and a reserve chief, who is also a lieutenant. We only operate three shifts with one reserve chief. We also have a sheriff and an undersheriff. This department has too many lieutenants. One lieutenant will have to go!"

TG thought to herself, "*I was right.*" The sheriff's announcement caused dismay among the wives and girlfriends of the lieutenants. Alarm quickly turned to joy as Sheriff Tom pointed at Jerry Burkley, and proudly promoted Jerry to his new rank. "I take great pleasure in announcing Lieutenant Jerry R. Burkley is now Captain Jerry R. Burkley."

Cheryl got applause when she asked Big Tom, "does that include a pay raise too?" Her question went unanswered.

24

Captain Burkley moved the celebration to Desmond's Pizza. Nobody seems to know who Desmond is, or was, nor how the Pizza Place started. It was one of those iconic eating establishments that had always been on Downey Street. Dewey Zolnozki, the long-time proprietor, preferred law enforcement customers. The feeling was reciprocal. Desmond's was a cop bar! Dewey's only standing rule was '*officers in uniform – back room.*'

Before Jerry sent on-duty deputies to the spacious rear room, he announced to all. "Separate checks for meals, soft-drinks or water if on duty, or within eight hours of duty. Beer and wine on me for others; hard drinks on your own."

"See!" said Big Tom to Edna. "I knew he was an excellent leader. No alcohol breath or impaired duty deputies. No unreasonable personal cost to wet down his tracks (a reference to the shape of captain's insignia of rank), and everyone knows what Jerry expects."

Edna patted Tom's arm and observed. "Kind of proud of your '*son*' aren't you?" Edna knew Tom thought of Jerry as the son they never had. So, did she!

Someone once observed 'crooks are stupid' Otherwise, we wouldn't catch them! David Kelly was a prime example. Kelly entered Desmond's with a revolver stuck in the front of his pants. Ninety-eight percent of Dewey's patrons present were sheriff's deputies, their wives or girlfriends, or civilians who were employed by Banner County Sheriff's Department.

Willy Harold noticed David Kelly look around and advance to the cash register, rather than go to an available table. Willy J grabbed a pitcher of iced tea and strode next to Kelly. About then, Kelly demanded money from Dewey Zolnozki and reached for the .357 magnum pistol at his waist. Willy dumped the pitcher over Kelly's head, and with his right hand grasped the gun around the cylinder to prevent the hammer from dropping. As he pulled the firearm from Kelly's grip, two other deputies clasped Kelly's arms, raising him against the desk. "Cuff's!" requested Willy.

Uniformed deputies transported David Kelly to the jail. Only 'stupid' robbers go to a place frequented by law-enforcement officers, let alone a location full of sheriff's deputies, to intentially commit a crime. Several of Kelly's cellmates repeatedly reminded David Kelly how smart he wasn't.

Day two for the record team began late. Due, in past, to Jerry's 'wetting down' celebration. The practice of wetting down the bars comes from the United States Army. Tradition dictates a newly promoted officer buy drinks for other members of the unit. Jerry had purchased many drinks for many thirsty friends in the past, as he gained promotions in the military. Jerry started as a warrant officer or warrant officer junior grade. He was subsequently promoted to warrant officer2, 3, and 4. Jerry has been selected for promotion to warrant officer5. WO5 is the highest warrant officer grade in the United States Army. All of Jerry's promotions had been represented by a single bar. Now Jerry Burkley would wear the double bar 'railroad tracks' of a captain. Jerry felt ecstatic. It showed on his face and by his demeanor.

The arrest of David Kelly by his patrol officers was the icing on the cake! It was a great start to a new chapter in Jerry's career

"Lieutenant - - sorry, Captain, phone for you on line two," called his secretary.

"Captain Burkley speaking!"

"Hi, Jerry, John Burks. Congratulations on your promotion."

"Thank you, Sir. What can I do for you today?" Jerry knew from experience a call from John R. Burks often meant a special mission for Jerry. This call was delightfully different!

"I want to give you a heads up. I'm going to run for President of the United States."

"That's awesome, Sir! What can I do to help?"

The phone call lasted two hours! The shout from Jerry's office even woke up Delta, the elderly Labrador retriever who faithfully served as a service dog for Molly Cook. Molly was the senior dispatcher. Delta slept under Molly's desk while Molly was working. Deputies loved Delta and would take the black Lab on potty breaks, and play with him. Jerry shouted, "Burks is running for President of the United States." Delta jumped to his feet, ran around in circles and barked (which he never did). Delta felt the joyous mood Jerry's announcement produced.

The substance of the next news was not as joyous but electrifying to the investigators. "Captain, sorry to interrupt," Rios Rivera told Jerry. "Laramie County Sheriff's Office just phoned. They have a DB (dead body) that may have the same COD (cause of death) as our Elmer Palmer."

"What do they have?" Jerry asked.

"A male who died of asphyxiation in an abandoned meat locker. The freezer still worked. No prints because the hands and feet were burned to a crisp!"

"So how is this DB connected to Palmer?"

"Alphabet soup agencies are inquiring. Laramie County remembered comments Sid (LT Sid Koslowski, BCSO) made in the all-agency briefing last week. This death would be two deaths with a federal interest. Deputy Taylor thought it was interesting. So do I." "Interesting call," said Judge Rio, the law west of the Rio (Rivera's nickname from Army friends in Vietnam).

"Follow-up," Jerry ordered.

About then Willie wandered in with Cheryl in tow. Molly's service dog, Delta, chasing after Willy excitedly. Delta and Willy were good friends because Willy always had a dog treat to feed Delta.

"Delta, sit." Delta sat.

"Good boy!"

Willy J gave Delta a doggy treat for obeying the sit command.

"Dog out. Deputy sit! What do you and my lovely wife need?" Jerry commanded.

"Lunch," stated Willy J.

"For you to look at house plans!" Cheryl exclaimed.

"And to help us look at the old courthouse and that spooky old funeral home," TG chimed in. "We have to look at both today. The empty warehouse isn't suitable. The judge, and I don't mean Judge Rios, but the one I work for, wants a quick decision. I'm not going into that scary mansion without you!"

OLD BUILDINGS

Jerry ordered, "Rusty Nail for lunch first! After lunch, we will look at the old, and end with frightening!"

"Great!" said Tashana (TG). "I'll call Carol and have her meet us at the Nail."

Only one dispatcher was on duty. The schedule listed two, but Andy Shepard was attending a mandatory training class. Molly Cook had everything under control. Her backup today, Sara Alzate, was out of the office on her lunch break. Molly had no control over one situation; her service dog. Molly had Parkinson's disease. Delta, a big, black Labrador, helped Molly with balance and other tasks. With Delta, Molly could do almost anything. What she couldn't do was operate the radios, phones, and take Delta for a needed potty break.

"Delta needs a walker!" Molly shouted. Three deputies, one booking clerk, and Tom appeared! All wanted to take Delta for his walk. Seniority prevailed. Sheriff Tom took Delta for his inspection tour of the lawn area. Finding a satisfactory location, Delta performed his 'break' effctively and with great relief. Big Tom then took Delta for a long walk. When they returned to dispatch, Delta went under the desk, laid down across Molly's feet, and went to sleep with a low snoring sound.

"You have a regal dog, Molly." said Tom.

"He's good to me too!" replied Molly.

"Me next." chimed in Sara. "Delta is such a nice boy. I love to walk him."

Jerry interrupted. "I will be with the record team (the nickname had stuck). We are going to the Nail for lunch, an inspection tour of the old courthouse, and then to see the 'spooky' funeral home. Tashana's description, not mine."

"In the log, Captain," replied Molly.

Soon the team was seated in a large booth at the Rusty Nail. Carol Ray arrived. Jerry inquired, "what is the rush on records movement?"

"The legislature is restructuring the court system once again. Banner County is getting a stand-alone district court rather than being part of the three-county district court designation we now share."

Cheryl looked puzzled. "I don't understand. We have two judges now. Why are we going to just one?"

The waitress appeared. Carol took charge. "Let's order; then I will give my lecture on Wyoming courts."

"Great suggestion, Carol." Jerry raised his hand and advised the young lady with an order pad and pencil ready, "I'll have the prime rib sandwich with fruit on the side, please!"

"Lunch is on Judge Broderick today, so feel free to order anything that looks good," suggested Carol.

"All our food is good," Julie Downs, the waitress, informed the team.

After everyone had placed their order, Carol rapped a fork on her water glass. "Class will now come to order! Wyoming court configuration has evolved since Wyoming became a territory to adapt to population shifts and changes in Wyoming laws and statutes. Wyoming Territory was created on July 25th, 1868. The Organizational Act created a supreme court with a chief judge and two associate judges. Those three judges were also the district judges for the original five Wyoming counties. When acting as a district judge, civil and criminal cases were heard by a single judge. If a case was appealed to the Supreme Court, all three judges ruled on the appeal. The standing joke was that from time to time, the judges assembled to approve each other's rulings."

Julie began serving lunch orders. Jerry took a bite of his sandwich, smiled, and commanded everyone to eat. "Carol can finish class later as we do our inspection tour."

Everyone dug in!

<<< >>>

The 'Old Courthouse' was a bust as a record storage facility. Lack of storage, limited space for court activities, and a deteriorating building, had been the justification for building a new structure for the court.

"I've seen enough," voiced Bill. "County would be better off building a vault for storage on the side of the new courthouse."

Carol continued, "let me finish my lecture. I think it will help clarify our mission."

Everyone found a place to sit or lean.

"As I was explaining, when Wyoming became a state in 1890, the new Constitution provided a separate supreme court, first with four judges and later with five as we now have. Wyoming only had five counties then, and three judicial districts."

"But we have thirty-three counties now!" observed TG.

"That's true, Tashana. Over the years, five counties became twenty-three. The legislature honored demands to divide several larger counties to serve changing population centers better. Five counties were split in half. Canyon and Banner were formally Canyon County. There are now thirty-three counties, but the judicial districts weren't changed." Some districts contain two or more counties.

"It's a real pain. Often there isn't a judge available for the court because the judge for that county lives in a different county," complained Willie. Attorneys, and others who had court business, often had to wait, or drive to another county to get a judge's signature on court orders.

"That is why the courts are being re-designated. Laramie County was the entire First Judicial District. Laramie County was divided into three counties, but all four district judges resided in Cheyenne (Laramie County). Each judge shared judicial duties in the other two counties. Each county will now get one judge, except Laramie County receiving two judges because the Capitol generates an additional caseload. All the other counties will be assigned one district judge, including Banner County. We get Judge Broderick. The court records for each county must be separated, remain intact for each respective court, and not combined in any one county's records. Thus, the need for storage space.

Jerry broke in. "Time to go to the spook house, I mean funeral home. Bud Hayes is waiting for us."

The stately building was a beautiful victorian castle, originally built as the personal home of an early territorial rancher. Known locally as the Grubb mansion, the residence had been the social center for many in Caribou. The top story is a ballroom with wood floors. Later the mansion functioned as a funeral home. The structure is a three-story stone building with cupolas and a winding porch around the front and side.

Carol's entourage; TG, Willy, Cheryl, and Jerry, were met at the bottom of the sandstone stairs leading up to the entrance. The gentleman standing on the bottom stair said, "my name is Hayes. I'm here to show you the premises and answer your questions." Bud Hayes was a distinguished gentleman dressed in a dark suit, starched white shirt, and dark red tie.

"Thank you, Mr. Hayes. We appreciate your time," Carol said, shaking the courtly man's hand. "Let me introduce you to my team."

"I believe I know them all. Mrs. Burkley was Cheryl Hefner when her parents lived in Caribou. Jerry and I have had professional dealings in the past. Willy J has done construction work for me, and I met Tashana at the courthouse when Judge Broderick asked me to stop by about this charming building. Welcome to you all."

Both Carol and Jerry were wondering if they had been set-up by the judge when Cheryl exclaimed, "yes, you used to work here, didn't you?"

"For twenty-six years. I was the senior embalmer and funeral director of Mountain Shadows Funeral Home in this historic building. This edifice was called the Grubb mansion when Mr. Grubb resided here. The mansion was then a funeral home, and has been vacant since the owner died four years ago and I retired."

Mr. Hayes led the group up to the full front stairs into a large room. In the center of the room is a massive staircase leading upwards and turning twice to allow access to the second floor. Walnut banisters with large knob posts line the stairs. Matching wainscots cover the lower half of the walls. An immense set of pocket doors give access to the other lower floor rooms. A small door leads to the side porch and basement access stairs.

"It's awesome!" said Cheryl. The others agreed.

"Why is it vacant?" asked TG.

"Some believe the building is haunted!" Teased, Mr. Hayes, with a grin. "It is a friendly bunch of poltergeists, though," Bud Hayes joked.

Mr. Hayes conducted the group around the first and second floor. Bud Hayes ascended a narrow set of steps to the third floor. The area is entirely open. The floors are polished wood planks. Dormer style full-length windows give light to the room, and a majestic view of the city.

Willy J announced, "if the building is sound and this floor will handle the weight, it would solve your storage and security needs. The building has office space on the first two floors. Willy intended to return later for a more thorough evaluation, but the records team was pleased with what they had seen.

<<< >>>

Jerry returned to his office, Molly was frantically waving him towards her desk.

"Does Delta need to go out?" Jerry asked.

"Delta's fine. You have ABCs in your office!"

"And who might they be?"

Molly was having fun with her captain. "Federal with several cryptic initials, and state with only three. FBI SAIC Cheyenne, and CID, also from Cheyenne. There is a rent-a-cop company rep in the lobby. The sheriff said to give them all to you. Lucky you!" Molly was giggling as Jerry walked to his office.

"Gentlemen, what can the sheriff and I do for you today?"

"Just checking on what information you have for us on Palmer," said FBI SAIC (Federal Bureau of Investigation Special Agent in Charge) Cheyenne, Zeke Flores.

"Who is us?" Jerry asked. "You and CID, you and the rest of your febbie crew, or you and some, as yet, unidentified alphabet agency such as the CIA?" Before Flores could even phrase an answer, Jerry informed the two bureaucrats, "probably about as much as your departments have shared with Banner County!"

"That's out of line deputy. Wyoming Criminal Investigation Division always cooperates with Wyoming law enforcement agencies!" retorted Carson Shoemacher, the CID director.

"First, if you haven't noticed, it's Captain, not deputy. Second, our department has received exactly nothing from your agency, even though we supplied CID with a copy of our entire case file, including pictures and diagrams. You now rank about even with the feebies for cooperation!"

The SAIC was indignant. "The title is Federal Bureau of Investigation, Captain. We are investigating a matter of national security, and your cooperation is mandatory."

Jerry rose from his chair, clamped his felt cowboy hat on his head and moved to leave his office. At the door, Jerry turned and advised the two astonished men, "when you have some information I might want to hear, call me on the phone or send an e-mail. Save you a long drive, and I might be inclined to assist you in your very, very, very important investigation. Banner County is engaged in our investigations."

Jerry hung his hat on a coat-hook and asked Sara Alzade to bring the rent-a-cop to the conference room. "Then have some deputies show the freeloaders in my office the way to the street, please."

Sara smiled and commented, "I will be pleased to carry out the mission, Captain!"

Saul Bernstein introduced himself to Captain Jerry Burkley. Saul was a salesman. His demeanor spoke volumes. A big grin, firm handshake, and cheerful greeting, demonstrated why he was also a successful manager. "My name is Bernstein, Sheriff! Thanks for seeing me. I represent GSI."

"My name is Burkley. I'm just a captain. The sheriff is tied up right now!"

"Sorry, Captain, you look like a sheriff. I won't take much of your time. GSI provides security for the Mountain Shadows Funeral Home property. Bud Hayes told me the sheriff's department was interested in leasing the property. GSI would like to continue our security services unless the sheriff is going to take over surveillance duties. If so, GSI would be pleased to assist in the transition."

"Thank you for both offers, Mr. Bernstein. The interested party is District Judge James Broderick. He is the district judge for Banner County. I was just helping take a first look at the building. You should see the judge. I'm not sure what his plans, if any, might be for the Grubb mansion."

CASH McCALL

Jennie, would you ask Glen, Jerry, Bob, and Carol Ray, to meet with me in the conference room at 1400 (2 PM), please?" requested Sheriff Flannigan.

"Sure! May I tell them why?" Jennie Abbote was Tom Flannigan's secretary. During the many years Jennie had assisted the sheriff she was usually aware of current projects or concerns. She had no idea of what subject the sheriff wanted to discuss with key staff.

The sheriff's answer didn't enlighten her. "Just tell them money!"

Jennie frowned. Big Tom grinned and went back into his office.

At the appointed time, all were present and seated around the conference table. Jennie was in attendance with pad, pencils, and a recorder. The sheriff thanked Jennie for her foresight. "I'm glad you could all attend. Sorry, I didn't mean to be cryptic, but the subject matter was not something I wanted disseminated, much less over the radio," began Tom. "Glen knows, because it was his hard work and dedication that make it possible."

"What is 'it'?" Jerry requested.

"Some new cars, light bars, sirens, and a department-wide encrypted, radio communications system! A base station, mobile, car, and hand-held portable radios, capable of interface with other agencies."

Carol observed, "I knew the radio system was approved in the budget. There isn't any money for the rest of your Christmas list!"

"Glen arranged money," Sheriff Tom announced with pleasure. "Glen, it's your turn!"

Tom sat, leaned back in his chair, and grinned ear-to-ear. Glen placed a poster on an easel and gave a short, concise, explanation of LEAA, a special federal fund for law enforcement agencies at the state and local level. "LEAA stands for Law Enforcement Assistance Administration. It is part of the Omnibus Crime Control Act of 1968. Money is given to the state for discretionary awards to local departments for training, communications equipment, and improved police equipment, to speed response times and public safety. We qualify in several areas."

"I don't hear police cars in your list," Carol pointed out.

"That's true. But as you noted earlier, we have money in the budget for communications radios. The county commissioners have agreed to let us use the communication funds for vehicles. LEAA will provide funds for an expanded communications system, as well as safety and response equipment such as light bars and sirens for the cars."

"Santa Claus!" quipped Bob.

"One might say," chuckled Tom as he re-assumed control of the meeting. "The cars have to be put out for bid. Carol, the sheriff's department will need your advice as County Attorney. Jerry, you oversee setting patrol car specifications and getting bids."

Discussions went on until early evening.

<<< >>>

Jerry and Tom were in the sheriff's office. Glen Marvin, Banner County Undersheriff, entered Tom's office and plopped into a chair. Glen was about to retire. His age and many years on the job working in law enforcement was beginning to show. Glen handled all the department's administration. Glen was a terrific 'paper pusher'. "I just got a teletype (electronic message) from Deputy Taylor in Cheyenne. Laramie County SO got an ID and cause of death on their dead body."

"Who was he?" asked Tom.

"How did they get an ID? I thought the hands and feet were burned," simultaneously inquired Jerry.

"Brian said they were able to use dental records. They match a missing person, Herman Story."

Sheriff Flannigan asked, "any connection to Palmer?"

"Not yet! Rios is working with Deputy Taylor on that issue," replied Undersheriff Marvin.

Jerry rose from his chair. "Sheriff, if you and Glen can do without my presence for a few hours, I have a date to teach Cheryl how to fly while I do my monthly qualification time in Sierra-Delta."

43

"Have fun. Don't bend my plane again!" Tom replied, referring to the dings and bullet holes incurred while Jerry was pursuing the Ferguson Federal Savings and Loan Bank robbers.

"Roger, Boss!" Jerry answered, giving the three-finger salute of a boy scout to his two superiors.

"Good man!" Glen noted after Jerry left.

"Yes, he is!" Big Tom agreed.

Over dinner that evening, Tom recited the conversation to Edna.

"Has Jerry figured out he is doing your job most of the time?"

"Hush, woman!"

Soon after Mountain Shadows Funeral Home closed, the building known as Grubb mansion was sold to new owners. The transaction was conducted in a shroud of secrecy. Libby Flats Trust put up the money. A title search only showed a chain of ficticious purchasers. The final registered deed listed Elfonzo Gutierrez as the owner.

The property was vacant four years. During that period, a vast underground evacuation (hole in the ground) was dug across the street. Those who asked were told it was a basement for a five-story building. Nothing was ever built on the site. Surreptitiously an underground room with rebar-reinforced walls, ceiling, and floor (a box) was fabricated and covered over. The area was subsequently paved over with asphalt and used as a parking lot.

One exit from the box, the only exit or entrance, was on the floor, or in the ceiling if you were in the room below). Under the box door was a small chamber. No egress from the vault existed until a tunnel was constructed from Mountain Shadow and connected to the underground vault. Impregnable steel doors secured access. After the tunnel shaft was completed, nothing was done for a long time.

Cheryl was excited. She was looking forward to her long-anticipated flying lessons with Jerry. After John Burks began campaigning for United States President, all of Jerry's free time was consumed assisting Senator Burks in Wyoming. None of the deputies, including Jerry, actively campaigned, since it might seem to conflict with their law enforcement duties. That didn't stop the wives and friends. 'Burks for President' campaign signs erupted like geysers in Yellowstone National Park. They popped up everywhere. Wives formed committees and got out the voters. The deputies were quiet, but active in the background. Before becoming a United States Senator from Oklahoma, John R. Burks had a long and distinguished military career. He retired as a general with four stars on his shoulders. Army veterans, and many military veterans from other military services knew Burks and liked him. By-election day all the local veterans had a chance to meet the 'General' in person. A twin-engine airplane was rented, and Jerry took his former commander on a whistle-stop tour of Wyoming. If there was an airport, there was a campaign stop. Law enforcement was there to applaud, not work. The primary election was over. John R. Burks won his party's nomination. Now Cheryl was going to get her first flying lesson.

"Ok, Pretty Lady. Get the plane out of the hangar, and I will show you how to do a pre-flight inspection," Jerry instructed Cheryl.

"Are you kidding me. No way can I push that thing out here!" Jerry's wife protested loudly.

Jerry laughed. "Why not? I do it all the time. Don't hit anything when you move the plane."

"No!! Way!!

Jerry led Cheryl into the large hanger, attached a tow bar to the front wheel, and plugged the electric motor cord into a nearby outlet. "It's easy. Watch!

"You're mean. You didn't tell me about the towing thing!"

Jerry kissed Cheryl and said, "you didn't ask!"

"True!" Cheryl kissed Jerry back.

Instruction now began in earnest. Jerry led Cheryl though a comprehensive walk-around inspection of the sheriff's department Cessna 206. "Usually you would start in a smaller, less complex plane, but this is one I use. Flying the 206 counts as mandatory qualification time for the month. Tom figured I could teach while I get my flight hours." Cheryl had flown with Jerry numerous times and knew how to buckle her seat belt. It felt strange to be on the left side of the airplane. Jerry sat on the right. He was comfortable in either position, whether fixed-wing or rotary-wing. He had many flying hours as an instructor and an incredible number as a pilot. Jerry patiently pointed out the various instruments on the panel before Cheryl and explained the use of each.

Finally, Jerry allowed Cheryl to start the engine. Jerry cracked his door open, and yelled "clear." Jerry nodded to Cheryl and she turned the key. The prop (propeller) began to turn and quickly became invisible. Cheryl soon learned taxi technique and guided the plane to the end of the active runway.

"All aircraft in vicinity of Caribou Airfield, November Three-Three-Sierra-Delta is moving to runway Two-Six for takeoff," announced Jerry over the radio's unicom frequency. Unicom is a frequency for airports without a control tower, to allow pilots to make their presence and intentions clear to other aircraft. Cheryl, with Jerry's assistance, taxied onto the runway, pushed the throttle forward, and began her takeoff run.

"Follow me on the controls," Jerry instructed. As the Cessna gained speed, Jerry eased back on the wheel, used the rudder pedals for alignment, the 206 lifted gently off the runway and became airborne. Cheryl was thrilled. She was handling the controls while the plane flew upward.

Jerry demonstrated the use of the flight controls once they had gained s safe altitude, and then let Cheryl experiment. Soon Cheryl was able to maintain a flight level, make turns, ascents, and descents, unassisted. The flight lasted a little over two hours. Cheryl was beat, physically and mentally, but extremely content. Jerry demonstrated the approach and landing to Caribou Field. On the radio, he communicated, "Three-Three-Sierra-Delta on final to Two-Six for landing." Jerry greased the landing and impressed Cheryl how smooth landing could be with an experienced pilot. She made a mental note she would learn to do the same.

Later, after the Cessna had been filled with fuel, and safely hangered, the two happy pilots adjourned to the Rusty Nail for a celebratory dinner.

"Guess what I did, Ed?" Cheryl happily asked Ed Plant, the owner of the Rusty Nail.

And, without waiting for an answer, blurted, "I flew an airplane!"

"Good for you!" Ed quipped. "Someone needs to be able to look after Jerry!"

"She's going to be a good pilot. She bored holes in the sky for two hours and didn't even bend the airplane," Jerry joked. "After being forced to ride with her all afternoon she wants me to buy her dinner too!"

Ed smiled. "That can be arranged as well. Come with me and I will get you started." Ed grabbed menus and escorted the happy pair to a corner table with a view of the fireplace.

"We don't need menus, Ed. Just order something delicious for us!" Cheryl exclaimed. "I don't want to waste time looking at a menu and making decisions."

Tom, a/k/a (also known as), Cash, owned Cash McCall Pontiac-Chevrolet. Tom often bragged, "you can save cash when you get in Cash McCall's cars!" Most of Tom's customers would agree. McCall sold new and used cars at a fair price, gave excellent service after the sale, and truly believed that a happy customer would not only buy another vehicle from him, but would bring their friends to buy!

McCall Pontiac-Chevrolet was also the only automobile dealer in Caribou, or for that matter, the only dealership in Banner County. That might account for the contract with Banner County to service all the sheriff patrol cars. Not driving round-trip to the next closest dealer justified the exclusive no-bid agreement.

Buying law enforcement equipped vehicles required, however, solicitation of bids from any dealer interested in selling a car, or even better, several cars for sheriff's department use, required the use of concise bidding procedures. Jerry determined what the department required.   Carol Ray determined the legal requirement. Carol and Jerry assembled a 'Request for Bids' package to be executed and filed by interested buyers.

THE USUAL 'Y' INCISION

Jerry's secretary advised. "Captain, Mr. McCall from Cash McCall's Pontiac-Chevrolet would like to visit with you."

"Send him in please."

Cash McCall entered Jerry's office and did something odd! Tom took off his ball-cap (which he rarely practiced). Cash sat in one of the comfortable office chairs before Jerry's desk and questioned Captain Burkley. "Is it true I got the contract for all the new cars and the Blazers too?" The Blazer is a Chevrolet four-wheel-drive utility vehicle, part car/part truck.

"If you can provide them equipped as specified and on schedule, I would say Yes. The order is for every vehicle at one time, not spaced apart." Jerry qualified. "We will also need garage space to install light bars, radios, and siren equipment, as outlined in the bid specifications."

Jerry had a good reason to solicit this information. Cash McCall operated out of a former gas station with a large metal building adjacent but behind the station. Jerry's prior investigation confirmed Tom was a successful proprietor of one of the larger dealerships in Wyoming. The sales and service structures weren't as convincing. Jerry and Tom were friends. They were both active Kiwanis Club members and donated time to various civic activities together. But this was business, not friendship.

Cash assured Jerry, "I have all the vehicles available, either factory direct or from other dealers. The contract can even be consummated sooner if you have the funds ready for payment. I can give you three service stalls 24-7."

"Great! Let's go to lunch and work out the details."

Willy J stopped Jerry on the way out of the building to advise, "The lumber yard will be delivering the first shipment of remodeling material to your place tomorrow morning."

"Outstanding!" Jerry commended Willy. What are they all laughing about in dispatch?"

"Molly has a tape of the big crime wave in Johnson county yesterday!" Willie laughed. "West of Buffalo, going up 16 to Ten Sleep is a roadside gas and convenience store. The manager hooked an extra speaker to his pa system and put it under the seat of the two-hole outhouse. Some lady with a long skirt entered, presumably to use the facility. The manager used his mike and announced. "Lady, please move over to the other side. I'm painting down here."

"How did that become a crime wave?" Cash asked.

"Well, the lady came running out without her skirt. Apparently, she had removed it before sitting on the wooden seat in the outhouse. When she came running out, she didn't have much on. It wasn't her lucky day! A Johnson County deputy drove into the area, and not knowing the circumstances arrested her for indecent exposure. Her husband objected and got detained for interference with a peace officer. Eventually, it all got sorted out, but in the interim, a backup unit also arrived and began operating with the same lack of information as the first deputy. The second deputy proceeded to round up the manager and the other customers, herd them into the coffee shop, and put it all out on the radio. That hapless deputy used the mutual aid channel to make his report. Everyone in the state could hear this crime wave unfold."

Jerry remarked, "there may be one hacked off sheriff someplace in Wyoming. Let's go to lunch."

Jerry and Cash McCall worked out all the new car transition details over lunch, including car colors. Carol promised to get the agreement on paper so the purchase could be concluded. Jerry was anxious to have the cars delivered. He intended to take the 'pick of the litter' for his patrol car.

Herman Story forced Sergeant Jack Falls and Doctor Henry Toshman to perform something neither would desire to do; drive to Cheyenne. Neither Jack nor Hank was a pilot. No pilot, no flying machine. Sheriff

Flannigan was insistent they determine the cause of Herman Story's death. Story's post-mortem examination should reveal that information. The sheriff trusted his staff and the professionals in Banner County. He had less confidence in other sources. His expectations of outsiders were meager! Tom Flannigan preferred to make his decisions in any criminal investigation based upon his own observations or from reliable information. Sheriff Flannigan felt comfortable having Jack and Doc T to be his 'eyes' for the autopsy. So the only option was to drive several hundred miles to Cheyenne.

With Sergeant Fells gone, Willie Harold, a senior reserve deputy, reported for duty.

"Willy J, thanks for coming in tonight," Lieutenant Pawlik told Sergeant Willie Harold. You are shift sergeant tonight. Jack's car is on the lot. Here are the keys."

"Thanks, Joe. I'll handle shift change and then get the building checks out of the way in case we get busy later.

Banner County Sheriff's Department routinely checked businesses, schools, and government buildings, to verify security and to check for any break-ins. Upon request from a homeowner, the same services were provided. The sheriff demanded his deputies take the moto, 'Serve and Protect' seriously.

"Outstanding. Thanks again for helping out tonight."

"No sweat! It's a marvelous change from my day job." responded Willy.

"How is Captain Burkley's, or should I say, Cheryl's, remodel job progressing?" Joe laughed.

"Cheryl's suggestions and requests are informational, and making the house look fine!" Jerry always gets in the last words, "yes, dear!"

Joe and Willy were laughing when the night dispatcher called to them. "I have an open-door silent alarm for the business at 206 South Buffalo. Who do you want me to send?" asked Jenny Abbote.

"Willy responded, "I'll take it, Joe, if you want to handle shift change. Less stress for both shifts."

OK, Willy. Hit the street."

The business located at 206 South Buffalo was named 'Two Critters'. The store was an underground gun-shop. Not clandestine, but in the basement of an unfinished building Burglars and sometimes plain daylight robbers were attracted to the location. Not because there were no bars on the windows – there were no windows. There were no windows on the two doors either. The store only had two entrances because the fire code demanded two exits from public places.

Firearms were securely housed in a large walk-in safe. The owner had a silent alarm connected to Banner County Sheriff Department Dispatch Center The front door opened into a large, well decorated and modern store. Willy J had spent many hours in the store admiring guns and law enforcement equipment; Willy had purchased his duty black basketweave leather gear at Two Critters.

The back entrance was a different world. From that door, small steps led down to a dark passage. "SO, Robert Two (Willy's reserve call-sign). On scene."

"Copy Robert Two. Do you need backup?" queried the radio dispatcher.

"Let me check the doors first."

"Robert Two, SO, 10-4 (radio code for OK)."

Sergeant Harold, retrieved his Kel-light, locked his patrol car, and walked to the Two Critters front door. Shinning his flashlight around produced the same information he observed using his patrol car spotlight driving in – nothing out of the ordinary.

"SO, Robert Two. Front secure. On my way to the rear door."

"Roger."

The reserve deputy sergeant perceived the next entrance was not only unlocked but partially open The adrenaline rush elevated Willy's pulse as he called this information to dispatch. "SO, Robert Two."

"Robert Two, SO."

"Back door open. I'm checking. I will take that back-up now!" Willie reported.

"On the way, Two," was Jenny's' calm response.

Willy J had been a reserve deputy sheriff since Sheriff Tom had initiated the concept several years before. Entering a dark building, with a possible intruder by himself, was Willy's first unaccompanied expedition into an unknown encounter with a criminal. As a deputy, Willy had worked solo many times and was always a single when supervising. Never had he walked into the dark alone. Other deputies had always been present.

"*What am I doing,* thought Willy?" He opened the door, shinning his Kel-light back and forth in front? He knew better than to advance without back-up but walked the steep stairs to the basement floor. No one jumped out or ran from him. Sweating under his kevlar vest, Willy checked out the entire basement area. He was standing by the open back door when Lieutenant Pawlik drove up.

"SO, Robert Two. All clear. Have the owner come and lock up!"

"Robert Two, SO. Copy."

Willie was part irritated and partly exhilarated. He was upset the owner of the business was so careless and quietly pleased with himself. Willy J had always wondered how he would perform in combat. Now, he knew, deep down, he would do whatever was needed. Some call it bravery. Cops, soldiers, and other first responders, call it 'being on the job'.

"Everything 10-4?" Joe asked.

"Couldn't be better," was Willy's calm reply,

The owner arrived to lock up his store. Willy didn't even give him the lecture he had rehearsed earlier as he traveled through the dark basement. The boost to his confidence overshadowed any desire to address the owner's deficiencies.

Autopsies usually end in a bland report. A recitation of all seen and deductions made by the pathologist based on the evidence presented comprised the final report. A post-mortem examination, especially for those watching the procedure for the first time, is memorable. Smells, never experienced, and observations of sights never seen or even imagined, remain for many years, if not forever. Even medical students remember their first exposure with disgust.

Sergeant Falls had seen many autopsies, or post-mortem examinations, during his law enforcement career. Now they just bored him.

Doctor T, on the other hand, was a pathologist. He was as interested in the post as a crossword addict was to a new puzzle. Indeed, Doctor T always viewed post-mortem exams as an answer to the mystery of what caused someone to die. He watched for evidence of motives, the why, as much as the how. Even natural causes had a 'why'; poor diet, addictions, etc. Murder cases were much more intriguing.

Hank and Doctor Simon Weaver had their heads together on this one. Sergeant Falls watched the beginning and then wandered around the premises. The autopsy was conducted at a local funeral home, which was general practice at the time.

The deputy was present to maintain a chain of evidence if anything relating to criminal charges was discovered. His job was to record who was present, receive, and store anything relevant to the ongoing investigation, and to verify an autopsy was performed.

This post began as all seemed to open, with a description of the body, and observations of abnormalities. Then the smell, strange odors, and sights start. As the pathologist would speak to the foot-operated recording device, "the usual Y incision was made."

SPECIAL MISSIONS

The sheriff shouted, "phone call on three, Captain."

"Jerry Burkley, how may I help you, Sir," Jerry said, reverting to old military habits, even though he didn't know who was calling. He never failed to answer calls the sheriff announced. Jerry knew Tom had pre-screened the caller. Jerry was pleased he had formally responded.

"Good afternoon, Jerry. This is John Burks.". Jerry didn't know the subject but hoped it was the campaign and not one of the Senator's 'missions' for him. The man calling was known, highly respected, and someone who was continually changing Jerry R. Burkley's life.

"Senator! Good afternoon, Sir! You know, you must stop changing your job title. I was about to say great to hear from you, Colonel. Anyway, yard signs are going up all over Banner County. Your staff has arranged for a Cessna 414 for me to take you to campaign locations. If there is an airport, we can probably get there!" Jerry was excited about the 'Burks for President' tour.

Burks quickly subdued Jerry's intensity for the presidential campaign. Senator Burks commenced, "simple mission this time, Jerry," the senator told Jerry. "I have a Navy Intel section with some very sophisticated communications equipment foreign nationals don't need to observe. The mission requires a National Guard Blackhawk to move a four-person team and a pile of equipment from Fort Carson, Colorado, to the Army National Guard hangar at the Cheyenne airport. The personnel will be three Navy and one Army plus 300 pounds of radio and antenna gear. Classified orders will follow."

"I assume you want me to fly the mission, Sir. Will I be using a 1022nd helicopter and crew?" Jerry inserted into the so-far one-sided conversation.

"That's affirmative. Orders naming you and three others will be hand-delivered to you in Caribou. The Intel team will be traveling with Wyoming Air National Guard medical communications units, and other units from across the United States, to the WINTEX (Winter Exercise) communications training in Germany. It is imperative the team appears to be part of the deployed Air Force medical units."

[Later, Jerry learned the Navy unit could listen to some heavily encrypted radio traffic from Russia and other Soviet Bloc countries. The Navy team, code name: X-Ray, provided expertise. The Army part of the group had the necessary electronics to enable the Navy intelligence technicians to spy on the Russians.]

Senator Burks closed the conversation with Jerry by observing, "just another drill weekend for you and your crew."

"Cowboy Two Zero, Salt Lake Center, descend to, and maintain, eight thousand feet on present heading. Contact Butts Army Airfield (Fort Carson, Colorado) on One-One-Eight-point Seven for landing instructions," a voice from the Blackhawk's radio intoned.

"Cowboy Two-Zero, copy. Have a great day, Center!" Rios advised the flight control center following their flight on the radar. MAJ Rivera changed the frequency on the primary radio, and transmitted, "Butts tower, Cowboy Two-Zero, a Blackhawk, due north for landing."

"Cowboy Two-Zero, cleared straight-in for landing on One-Eight. Follow taxi-way to the first hangar on the right."

"Cowboy Two-Zero, Roger."

The 1022nd Medical Company helicopter was soon parked adjacent to the large designated hangar. The four crew members offloaded and walked to a small door set into the sizeable sliding hangar door. The only visible items in the vast area were several pelican style plastic equipment boxes used to store electronic equipment in transit, and large canvas-covered bags of radio antennas. The older man perched upon the top of this massive pile had a visible name tag on his uniform embroidered 'CAPT S.X. Fordham'.

"Guy looks pretty old to be a captain; must have done something wrong," SPC4 Wing whispered.

"Look again," warned Major Rivera. "He's got eagles on his shoulders. That 'guy' is Navy. In your world, he's a full colonel."

Rios walked over to the captain and saluted. The captain did not return the salute. "Major Rivera, Sir, with three and a Blackhawk. Are you Quincy?"

"I am, and if I'm not mistaken, your or someone in your party, has information for me."

"Yes, Sir. Could I please see your I.D.?" It was more order than a question.

CAPT Fordham slid off the equipment pile and handed Rios an open black wallet containing impressive credentials.

Major Rivera turned, gestured to WO3 Burkley, and said, "Mr. Burkley, Captain Fordham is assigned to Operation Quincy!"

Jerry quickly stepped forward, examined the black wallet, and handed it back to Captain Fordham. Jerry first told Rios, "The Navy doesn't salute inside." The look on both Fordham's and Rivera's faces demonstrated WO3 Burkley had scored a minor victory.

"I understand you may have some mission documentation for me to review," Captain Fordham asked Warrant Officer Burkley.

Jerry zipped open a pocket on the leg of his flight suit. He removed a small canvas case and removed some documents.

"Sir, here is a copy of the mission order," and handed Captain Fordham two pieces of paper covered with transparent plastic. I presume your team all have proper clearance for this information."

"Yes, they do Mr. Burkley." Captain Fordham carefully read the document. "This will suffice, Mr. Burkley. Thanks for your assistance. Fordham passed the document to other team personnel. I want you all to see this, so you know who has a 'need to know' about this mission."

DEPARTMENT OF DEFENSE
UNITED STATES OF AMERICA
TOP SECRET/QUINCY
NFRFN
//
MISSION ORDER
OBJECTIVE: Insert Special Operations Team X-Ray
PERSONNEL ASSIGNED:
Fordham, Sidney Xavier, CAPT, USN, Force Intel.
Binger, Julius G., PO1, USN, NOS B600
Reed, Michael T., PO2, USN, NOS B600
Williams, Charles D., MSG, USA, MOS 35X.
Rivera, Rios NMI, MAJ, USA, AC 1022 Med Co WYARNG.
Burkley, Jerry R., WO3,USA,Pilot, 1022 Medical Co WYARNG
Davenport, Jackson, SSG ,Crew Chief, 1022 Med Co. WYARNG
Wing, Ronald C., SPC4, Medic, 1022 Medical Co. WYARNG
ASSIGNMENT: Carry out "OPERATION QUINCY," as directed.
TDY authorized all personnel assigned.
Mission assignments will be provided at QUINCY SIX discretion.
BY ORDER OF THE PRESIDENT OF THE UNITED STATES
S/BG THOMAS B. DEVINE
Secretary, Joint Chiefs of Staff
TOP SECRET/QUINCY
NRFN

[For the reader's information: NRFN means No Release to Foreign Nationals. TDY means temporary duty and authorizes quarters/pay for the military member.]

Soon the group gathered in a secure hangar room. The area was soundproof and hardened electronically to prevent any conversation from being heard by others outside. "Sir," Jerry addressed Captain Fordham, but allowed all present to listen. "I am Quincy 6. I know you, and several others present, outrank me. Senator John R. Burks, and subsequently the president, have designated me, to command this operation. I will not interfere with your assigned duties. My mission is to insert you, provide information and support, and get you back out again. It was determined I could better achieve that goal by having command. I am not accustomed to acting as commander. I am a warrant officer, but I hope we can all accommodate each other to successfully get our respective jobs done and get out of here in one piece."

Captain Fordham nodded. "I have no problem with what you have outlined so far."

Major Rivera seconded that notion, and commented, "Jerry, I mean Warrant Officer Burkley, has brought me back from more than one successful mission. I trust him, and I hope you will too."

Senator Burks had previously briefed Jerry on the mission details and the information to be communicated to team X-Ray. The senator began, as he had done in times past, "As usual, you will brief the mission team. Your helicopter with the 1022nd Medical Company call, 'Cowboy Two-Zero' will proceed to Fort Carson, Colorado. You will find the the other X-Ray team members and equipment. Brief the team, including your crew, and transport the group and equipment to the Wyoming Air

National Guard/Wyoming Army National Guard area of the Cheyenne, Wyoming, airport. Land at the 1022nd, as you usually would. The 187th Aeromedical Evacuation Squadron will move the equipment by field ambulances and stretchers as simulated patients to the departure area.

"Why not just have the Carson group taken directly to Cheyenne?" Jerry asked.

"Wyoming Army National Guard helicopters will blend in at Carson. Air Force or Navy aircraft at Carson might draw attention we don't want. This team would be an assassination threat if identified," replied the senator.

Senator Burks continued, "take the team to an Air Force unit deploying to the Winter Exercise (Communications) in Germany. It is imperative the group appears to be part of the WINTEX exercise and not an active duty Naval Intelligence unit. The Air National Guard units will all be Medical Service Corps officers and radio operators.

Jerry briefed the team as he had been informed and instructed, including the Senator's closing remarks. "Oh, when X-Ray is mission complete, I need your assistance moving the team back to Fort Carson."

Do we return in two weeks, or RON in Cheyenne?" Jerry asked.

"I want you available to support the team in Germany. You will deploy to Donaueschingen, Germany and be quartered at the Hotel Zur Sonne, as will the rest of the team. All the necessary arrangements are made. Major Rivera is a Medical Service Corps officer, you are a medical evacuation helicopter pilot, and SPC4 Wing is a medic. You should fit right in. Have a nice vacation."

Sure, thought Jerry – memories of other 'simple' missions from John R. Burks quickly remembered!

Eventually, all the WINTEX personnel and equipment arrived in Germany. It had been a long excursion on C-130 and C-141 aircraft. The X-Ray team was met by a young Air Force first lieutenant, "Sir, I am Lieutenant Trevor Smith. Welcome to Donaueschingen! I have transportation for you and your equipment. Let's get it loaded, and I will brief you as we drive. We have about a two-hour drive. I would like to have you all settled in before dark."

"That sounds like a plan Lieutenant," acknowledged Rios. There are eight of us, and about six hundred pounds.

"Not a problem, Sir. I have a Mercedes van and a three-quarter-ton stake truck."

Captain Fordham was wearing the uniform of an Army warrant officer two. Most military members, if they thought of it at all, would assume his warrant was a late-career promotion for having performed well as a radio technician. Master Sergeant Williams was wearing his standard Army field uniform. The other two Navy team members were wearing Army fatigues with Army rank insignia that matched their Navy pay grades. To observers, everyone appeared to be Army radio communications and operations supervisors.

Fordham directed the loading of the ¾ ton truck. He and Williams rode in the cab with the enlisted supply specialist from their host unit.

First Lieutenant Smith was the commander of a contingency hospital at Donaueschingen. He commanded six enlisted supply specialists and a German civilian secretary. The hospital had no doctors, nurses, or other medical personnel. In the event the hospital was activated as a medical treatment facility (a contingency), medical staff would be sent from Reserve and National Guard units. The lieutenant's job was to keep the hospital supplied with fresh medical supplies and store them until near their expiration dates. At that time, Lieutenant Smith and his six supply warriors would ship the supplies to an existing medical facility for use and stock the contingency hospital with fresh supplies to be available if activated.

"Major Rivera," Lieutenant Smith explained as they drove down the Autobahn (a four-lane divided highway like a U.S. Interstate), "none of us live at the hospital. Costs too much to heat a whole wing for just seven of us. We all live on the 'economy' (slang for renting quarters from a German landlord). I have arranged rooms for you at the Hotel Zur Sonne. This Mercedes van is a rental for your use. The hospital only has the truck for transportation."

"Interesting," Jerry commented. "It does sound like a vacation."

"The hospital will be available for your use during WINTEX." Lieutenant Smith said, almost wiping the grin off Jerry's face, but not quite.

Molly Cook had been employed by the Banner County Sheriff's Department longer than anyone. Most Caribou residents assumed Big Tom had come with the department as part of the original issue. Molly was already a fixture when Tom was a new deputy.

Undersheriff Glen Marvin was on the telephone with Molly's only child, Tammy Fitzgerald. "Glen, Molly passed over last night. Mom said she was mighty tired and went to bed early. I'm so glad I was with her all week."

"Tammy, I'm so sorry. What can the department or I do to help? Molly was family to everyone here," consoled Glen.

"The funeral will be at Larimore's on Wednesday at two p.m. The department personnel are invited. Please let everyone know."

"I will. Please call me if you need anything or want help."

Glen could hear the tears in Tammy's choked voice as she informed him, "nothing now, maybe later."

Glen Marin put his phone back in the cradle and walked to Sheriff Flannigan's office across the hall from his. "Bad news, Tom. Molly died last night. Her daughter, Tammy, said Molly was tired, went to bed, and never woke up."

"Does Tammy need the department to do anything?" Big Tom inquired.

"No, Sir," Glen reported. "Just to be at the funeral and the reception after."

"You can be sure we will be there. Put out at each shift change that I expect every Banner County Sheriff's Department employee not on duty to be present in dress, not patrol uniform, attire."

The funeral service was conducted at Larimore Funeral Home by Bud Hayes. Bud and Molly were old friends. Amazing Grace was sung by Velma Shepherd, accompanied by three guitar players from the Caribou High School concert band.

Bud escorted the family members to the reception area, returned and dismissed those in attendance, row-by-row, and superintended the reception.

Tom Flannigan was holding a cup of coffee in one hand and two sugar cookies in the other. "Sheriff," Tammy Fitzgerald informed Tom, "Delta needs a new home." Tammy was asking for help. Molly had been Tom's first dispatcher. Molly had a service dog named 'Delta.' Delta was a black Labrador who accompanied Molly to work every day. Molly had Parkinson's disease and balance problems. Delta provided support to prevent falls, and assistance in getting back on her feet if Molly did fall. Everyone who saw the loyal service dog commented on his regal stature. Delta crawled under the desk while Molly was working. Deputies almost stood in line to take Delta for a walk, even if they might have to pick up dog poo in a plastic newspaper bag.

"No reason Delta can't hang around here. He's too old to continue his job for someone else. I'll take him to my place nights, and he can lay around the office as he has always done. Be a good retirement for him!"

"Thanks, Sheriff. Molly and Delta would both like that." Tammy hugged Tom and handed him the leash. Tammy had happy tears running down her cheeks.

"Since we now have a K-9 Division, maybe we need a K-9 officer," suggested Sara Alzate. Sara's husband was a sheep rancher, and one of the Sheriff's reserve deputies.

"Good idea!" said a grinning Willie J. "and maybe a K-9 police dog too. All Delta does is sleep, eat, and poo."

Everyone present laughed. That evening Tom told Edna, "a police K-9 might be a good idea."

Edna responded, "If you can find the right dog, a trainer, and a K-9 officer; all you would need is a pot of money. Maybe you can win the lottery."

On that note, Tom and Edna retired for the night.

LIBBY FLATS

Doctor Robert Weisberg and Willy J were having a late lunch at the Moose. Both were drinking iced tea and eating a steak sandwich. Their far ranging conversations turned to a subject near and dear to most Wyoming residents.

"Where are we going deer hunting this fall? Doctor W challenged Willy.

"Well, Doc, I ran into a fellow last week who was enthusiastic about Libby Flats over by Centennial. Of course, he was still drunk, had rolled his pickup, and not thinking clearly. His idea of a good hunt may depend on finding beer instead of deer!"

"Haw," guffawed Weisberg. "Maybe we should look into it anyway. I think that area is in Medicine Bow National Forest and that the road across the top through Libby Flats is closed in the winter. Might be good hunting if we were to take horses."

There was more to discuss on this subject, but Banner County Sheriff's Department dispatch interrupted. "Robert Two, SO."

"SO, Robert Two bye!"

"Robert Two, assist Charlie Forty. Domestic disturbance, Seven-Six-Nine Chimney Rock Road."

"Copy SO, on the way," Willy transmitted. Willy stood, pushed his half-eaten sandwich away, and informed Doctor Weisberg, "thanks for lunch. I'll pay you later!" Willy then ran to his patrol car, activated the emergency lights on the overhead bar, and went to back up Chris Roads.

The Hotel Zur Sonne has ten hotel rooms for rent, a bar, and a superb restaurant. Jerry's team occupied eight of the ten hotel rooms. Jerry and his little group were welcomed by the Zur Sonne owner and his family.

Father, mother, grandmother, and two teenaged children, ran the hotel operation as a team. Grandmother supervised the daily continental breakfast (bread, rolls, lunch meat, assorted cheese, juice, coffee, and water). Unfortunately, grandmother did not speak English. She was, however, adept at gestures and could sense what a customer may need or desire. Father handled cooking, the children cleaned rooms, and mother oversaw everything else, including the bar.

Lieutenant Smith's hospital was a former rest and recreation center for the Nazi Wehrmacht officers during WWII. The bottom or basement level was a horse stable, now transformed into a medical supply warehouse. The first level contains elaborate offices, a conference room, and maintenance areas to repair medical equipment. The stately building is three stories in height, with an attic space under the roof. Each of the lower stories is two stories tall. Each room has huge floor-to-ceiling windows and access to the wrap-around balcony. The attic is a full-story tall and provides additional storage areas. The building is the shape of a 'U.' Each room has a glorious view. The view is fantastic in every direction as a result of having been erected on top of the tallest hill in the area.

"What do you think of the Hotel Zur Sonne, Mr. Burkley?" asked Lieutenant Smith. "Duvet and a bottom sheet. Cozy once you get accustomed to the arrangement. Nice shower after I figured out how to turn on the water heater in the room, a radio, and a great view of the Fürstenberg Brewery," gushed Jerry.

The team organized into two seprate but connected routines. Sidney Xavier Fordham and his covert intelligence operation had moved their activities into one of the maintenance areas on the ground floor (and a long walk from the lieutenant's office area and the conference room). The elaborate computer-assisted communications surveillance gear and radio equipment was arrayed in vertical stacks. Coax cable ran out the door, through the halls, and up to the attic. In the enclosed attic area, the coax was attached to multiple antennas (somewhat like satellite dishes used on houses). None of this complicated installation was visible from outside the hospital building.

The radio communication antennas used by the WINTEX team were prominent. Jerry and his team, with Sergeant Williams' assistance, hung outside an attic window a massive folded dipole antenna. The antenna was strung from the attic window to each upper end of the u-shaped window, forming a large v. (A dipole antenna is two long horizontal cables with short vertical wires connecting the two long cables every few feet. A coax cable is attached to the middle section of the antenna and dropped down the side of the building into the conference room.) An encryption capable high frequency, shortwave, two-way radio rested on the center of the conference room table. This equipment comprised the WINTEX communications center.

"Pretty slick, Sir!" Jerry congratulated the Navy captain dressed in army fatigues. "Your system is clandestine, mine is overtly obvious and will account for any rfi (radio frequency interference) you may create."

"You're pretty slick too, Mr. Burkley, for an Army warrant officer!" exclaimed Sidney.

"Well, at the moment, you are an Army warrant officer too," Jerry laughed.

Rios joined the mutual admiration society. "Did you know, Sir, the Navy doesn't have any warrant officers?"

"We used to have some many years ago. The Navy discovered we didn't need them," replied Sidney Fordham.

Everyone laughed.

Captain Fordham turned serious. "Mr. Burkley, you and Major Rivera are also law enforcement officers, are you not." It was a statement of fact, not a question.

"We are, Sir," responded Rios. "I am a deputy with Banner County Sheriff's Department in Wyoming, and Mr. Burkley is a captain."

"Well, captain! That sounds much nicer than Mr. Perhaps you can both help our mission in that capacity. We are picking up some interesting chatter we don't fully understand. You are both welcome to come to listen with us. Maybe you can give us a different point of view. Even if you can't, I think you will find it interesting. I'll send Sergeant Williams to the conference room to cover your net."

"Thank you, Sir. We would like that," Rios answered.

"All right!" Jerry smiled. "Cops and robbers!"

"More like spies and counterspies. Or maybe just a computer game," dourly replied Captain Fordham.

Libby Flats is not flat. The area is at the top of a high ridge in south-central Wyoming. The wind and snow have made strange shapes of the few trees, bent out at weird angles away from the wind. Of course, that is most of Wyoming; the air is always on the move, generally from the north-west. Most residents have remarked, "It would be a nice day if it weren't for the wind."

Banner County was blessed. Mountain peaks with snow on the tops most of the year, towered over green valleys, with lakes reflecting mountain tops. The mountain tops blocked the air currents and directed the air over the valleys. Nature had made Caribou a great place to live and work.

Libby Flats, however, was home turf to the trust with the same name. Libby Flats was close to Centennial, Wyoming, where the board held meetings. The board owned several sections. [A section is 640 acres; one acre is one mile on each side of a square.] The board's primary interest involved property far north of Libby Flats, but still in Wyoming.

"The board will come to order," announced Dr. Fredrick Richmond. The other members of the board; George Smith, Kalinda Canton, Jim Feltner, Delmar Bushmill, and Helen Palmer, were seated around a large conference table. Two members of the board, Elmer Palmer and Herman Story, were absent. Those in attendance were all attentive and ready for this meeting to begin. Present were the directors of Libby Flats Trust Foundation. This foundation had no connection with the area in Wyoming called 'Libby Flats', a scenic, but desolate area between Centennial and Saratoga, Wyoming. The board met in Centennial, Wyoming, at the Mountain View Hotel, because it was close to real estate owned by the trust and was convenient for the board members. The foundation land was not far from the open mountain area called Libby Flats. The board had other properties and interests. The board had several essential items to discuss today. The 'Notice of Meeting' listed them as:

Libby Flats
CW
Caribou Storage/maintenance
GSI

After opening formalities, George Smith raised his voice and asked, "who, or what, is GSI?"

"Be patient, my friend. All will become clear as we progress," responded Dr. Richmond.

"Ok but make it quick!"

Others vocally joined Smith in demanding an answer. The gavel banged. "All in order or leave," commanded Dr. Richmond. "This meeting will be conducted as outlined in the official announcement."

All the board members were very aware Fredrick Richmond did not countenance obstructions to his meetings. All were quiet and seated when Dr. Richmond pronounced, "the first order of business is to determine Story's location. We know Palmer is dead. Where is Story?"

Kalinda Canton, a board member from Canyon County, offered, "I thought he went to Cheyenne to meet with ---."

"Quiet," said Jim Feltner. "Don't use names."

"All right- Story went to Cheyenne."

"Anyone else," requested Dr. Richmond. "We will continue looking at Cheyenne until we learn otherwise. Remember, Story and Palmer both have tunnel information."

The meeting moved on slowly as most board meetings have a tendency. "Our next order of business is CW. We will discuss that when we take up GSI."

"What's CW?" asked Delmar Bushmill, the newest board member.

"You can think of him as Cecil or CW. No other information will be provided at this time. See me later for briefing," stated Dr. Richmond.

Dr. Richmond moved on to the next item on the agenda. "Caribou. Our storage facility in Caribou, Wyoming, may be compromised. Suggestions?"

The board considered options for several hours, then took a lunch break. The food was good, the drinks better.

After lunch, President Richmond called the meeting back into session. "Caribou Storage is not yet resolved."

"Move continuance," said a bored, board member, Jim Felner.

The motion was seconded and quickly passed. This decision might haunt the Libby Flats Board later.

Finally, the board began to discuss GSI. GSI was an eye-opener for all the board members, except Dr. Richmond.

GSI was, and is, a private security firm, but not the typical business entity. GSI was entirely owned, operated and controlled, by an obscure United States Government Agency. Neither the public nor most government officials were aware of GSI's existence. Most members of Congress, who annually approved the lavish budget, did not know the agency's purpose. Some military leaders were given limited insight into the agency's activities, but only after a demonstrated 'need to know'. The agency is generally known as 'Global Security Insurance', which was also a code name for GSI. The title passed unnoticed in most revenue bills considered by Congress. No federal laws established or authorized GSI. Money from the United States Government made it a viable organization with no oversight. GSI was the ingenious invention of a few men and women who wanted to control.

Outsiders, including the Libby Flats Board, thought GSI stood for 'Global Security Incorporated'. That too was an apt cover name.

"GSI believes an American may know information about your vault and the tunnel access," Saul Bernstein told the assembled Libby Flats board members. Saul was the public figure for GSI.

"How do you know?"

Saul turned to Lamar Robinson and replied, "GSI does your security. We are a large organization and have many assets in the field. The question is, what does this board want GSI to do?"

Dr. Richmond advised Saul, "The board will discuss options and advise GSI later." Saul Bernstein left the room.

"This is where CW, our missing board members, and Caribou storage, affect Libby Flats," cautioned Dr. Richmond.

Willy J and Doctor W started planning their hunt at Libby Flats. Both created lists of what was needed, what could be borrowed from others, and what had to be purchased. It kept them busy in their spare time!

Rios and Jerry were similarly occupied, but for different reasons. Master Sergeant Williams was becoming part of the WINTEX team, handling the simulated radio message traffic. [The process of encrypting radio messages involved typing the transmission in a prescribed format on a small keyboard connected to the radio transmitter. Buttons pushed on the little keyboard box created a random code, scrambling the letters and characters. Pushing another switch would allow the radio to transmit the message over the air in a quick burst. A similar box on the receiving end could decode the signal and print the message in plain language. Voice contact on both radios was required so the radios could then communicate with each other.]

Master Sergeant Williams knocked on the conference room door, and then entered. "Morning gentlemen. Captain Fordham said you need to come and listen. The tunnel guys are on the air."

"Thanks, Sarge! The message is in the box and ready to go," Major Rivera informed Chuck. (both teams were now on a first-name basis.)

Rios and Jerry sat opposite a large rack of radio receivers in chairs 'borrowed' from 1LT Trevor Smith's fancy office. (A one or two-star general would occupy the office if the hospital was activated. The furniture was for the general, not the lieutenant.)

"What have you got for us, Sid?" Jerry asked as he reached for a headset. Neither Jerry nor Rios spoke or understood any of the languages transmitted. The computers and Fordham's specialists translated the conversations into English and made written transcripts. Those listening to the recorded messages could read along and then understand what was said. The actual voices provided inflections and meaning to the transcript text.

"Listen, then we will talk," Captain Fordham suggested. Both lawmen put on headphones, slid notepads close, and listened intently.

"Sheriff," Willy pried. "Are you serious about a K-9 police dog?"

"Seriously considering it, why?"

"Rios is from Casa Grande, Arizona. The Judge knows a former Air Force K-9 handler, Louis Robinson, who lives near Casa Grande. Robinson trains dogs professionally. He has a reputation for being a superb teacher. He instructs the dog and the handler at the same time, so they become a team."

"That sounds intriguing, but we don't have a dog yet! Delta is too old to re-train."

"Delta's AKC (American Kennel Club) registration has the breeder's name, Sloan Island Labradors, on the certificate. The breeder, or Robinson Dog Training, could help us find an appropriate dog." Willy was on a roll. "Then all we would need is a K-9 officer."

"Sure, and money in the budget to pay for the dog, training for the dog and the officer, equipment, salary for the new hire, and miscellaneous other expenses."

"Hey, Sheriff. If all that could be worked out, what would you want the dog trained to do?"

"Willie J, I hope that was a rhetorical question. The suggestion of a department K-9 didn't address that issue. Don't know what a police dog can do, much less why we need another dog who 'eats, sleeps, and poos'. Beats me how a police dog would earn his keep." Tom put on his hat and started to take Delta, who was sleeping on his feet, for a walk.

Willy J then goofed. "Louis said we should train him as a police patrol dog." Just then, Willy realized what he had done and shut up!

The Sheriff turned and glared at Willy. "Just who all is involved with this great K-9 aquisition campaign?"

"Most of the department. It just seemed like a great way to honor Molly. And from what Louis told us, a dog could be a real asset to a rural law enforcement agency."

"I assume 'Louis' is Robinson Dog Training. What else did he suggest? By the way, who contacted Louis? Or did he approach you?" Tom was starting to show signs of anger.

"No, Sir. Louis didn't contact us until after Edna called him. Then Louis called for Rios, but he wasn't here because he's with Jerry in Germany for the senator."

Sheriff Tom Flannigan was beginning to get confused, but he sensed the department was going to gain a K-9. "Sit back down Deputy Harold and start over from the beginning," the sheriff ordered.

"Yes, Sir. A few days ago, Mrs. Flannigan called Rios Rivera in Germany. She asked him if he knew about the suggestion to have a department police dog. He not only said yes, but told your wife about Louis Robinson. She called Robinson. During their conversation, Mr. Robinson suggested looking at the AKC certificate. Then your wife called me. I called Mr. Robinson, and we visited at great length about police dogs in general, and what specifically this department could expect to achieve ."

Sheriff Tom made a 'come on' gesture with both hands. Willy continued, "Louis suggested training the dog to be a patrol dog who could ride along in a car, protect the deputy, and out of the unit, subdue criminals, and assist in finding suspects at the scene. Primarily the dog would be trained in protecting and apprehension. He also mentioned that a good patrol dog was a fabulous public relations tool. Most kids would like to pet the dog, and parents would beam, and identify favorably with our department, or something like that."

"Ok, deputy. Get out of my office. And thanks! I appreciate your input and the stress I just put on you." (Willy J had expected the sheriff's response. Edna had advised him how to approach Big Tom, what to do, and what to expect. Willy had been carefully briefed.)

Tom went home to have a long talk with Edna. (Tom talked Edna suggested.) Then he advised the department staff a new K-9 might (would) join the department if (when) a suitable K-9 officer and K-9 were obtained. Tom had long experience in which battles to fight, and when to give in gracefully. Besides, Delta needed a buddy!

"Willy J, I have a project for you."

"Sure, what's up. I am up to date on Cheryl's remodel and waiting for Jerry to return and approve, so I have lots of free time."

"Call that lake breeder and find us a dog!

"It's Sloan Island Labradors. Although I think they may have a lake. I'm on it, Boss." Willy bounced out of the sheriff's office. In the dispatch office, Willy J said, "guess what? The heriff's office is getting a K-9."

Cheers and clapping followed his announcement.

Willy then used his cell phone to call Germany!

FALSE ALARM

Jerry, Rios, Chuck and Sid, had listened to the transcript .tapes three times; once together, one time solo, and again together. Scribbled notes filled notepads. Captain Fordham suggested, "let's go around the table (the group was seated around the conference table at the 652nd U.S. Air Force Contingency Hospital in Donaueschingen, Germany). Captain Fordham's mission was to intercept radio transmissions and analyze the data to determine if it affected the national security of the United States. "My team is stymied about the significance of what is being said on the tapes," Sid admitted. "I am hoping you can shed some light on the relevance. Quite frankly, I have no idea if, or how, this information might be of value. I would hate to miss something that would affect national security or any of our people."Jerry summarized. "The dialog seems to concern three or four major issues:

First; computers, or a specialized computer.

Second; a tunnel or shaft.

Third; a safe or vault.

And finally; a missing attorney or someone else. Maybe a contact or associate.

Rios and I couldn't discern any other fact indications. Someone talked about something 'flat', but nothing else rang a bell, flat or not. Sorry, Sid, we didn't see anything else. They appeared to be talking around subjects. We didn't hear anything else. Maybe if we saw something we could contribute more."

"Captain, and I say that with great respect. You and Deputy Rivera are extremely conscientious in your investigation of our quandary. Unfortunately, we reached the same non-resolution."

"In my experience in law-enforcement, Captain Fordham, I have discovered that letting the evidence simmer sometimes allows the answer to come when something else is heard or observed," Jerry advised Sid.

"I will forward the report, together with a follow-up recommendation. Thanks very much for your assistance."

"Proud to help you anytime. Rios and I are honored to be allowed to participate in your activities. Please contact me if there is anything else we can do for the Navy. If you will get your gear packed up and out front, I can perform one last mission for all of us; get us home."

Captain Fordham smiled and advised Jerry, "if you return Master Sergeant Williams to us, we would be pleased to assist him in 'packing up HIS equipment'!"

The retro-deployment was the reverse of the deployment. Everyone was soon delivered back to where each started the journey to WINTEX.

Before the team departed Donaueschingen, and the Hotel Zur Sonne, Captain Fordham, Major Rivera, and WO3 Burkley hosted a farewell party for the Army/Navy team, the Air Force personnel and spouses of the 652nd Contingency Hospital (the host unit for the WINTEX team), and the family and friends of the Hotel Zur Sonne owners.

All the invitees attended the celebration. Soon a plastic boot filled with Fürstenberg beer was passed around each table. Most of those in attendance were aware of the awesome power and danger or drinking from the unique drinking vessel. Those who were not aware quickly learned. When the beer level in the boot got below the toe, there was a danger to the person drinking the beer as the boot vessel was tipped back to drink. The sticky beer would gush past the air bubble between the toe and the heel, awarding the partaker a swift face of Fürstenberg. Captain Fordham and Master Sergeant Williams received the first two showers. Others soon experienced the surprise shower. The guests had a choice. Drink and take a chance or go thirsty.

Jerry was seated between Herr Max and his wife, Gretchen, the proprietors of Zur Sonne. Both spoke impeccable English from having spent summer vacations in the United States. The conversation became intriguing to Jerry.

Max's wife leaned forward to speak past Jerry and said to Max, who was seated on Jerry's other side, "whatever became of our guest who never checked out and left everything in the room Mr. Burkley is occupying?"

"Yah, I remember the American. He was quiet, walked around a lot, but always seemed to eat and sometimes drink here. He didn't have a party like this. I don't know. He just never showed up one day. I helped the girls put his things in storage. I told the Detectiv (German for Detective), but I don't believe he did much. Why do you ask?"

"I thought you might have heard. None of our local patrons mentioned anything. He was a nice man. So is Jerry. Jerry is using the same room, and that just jogged my memory."

At the time, the information didn't mean anything for Jerry. Late that night, Burkley awoke. He had been dreaming of or thinking about the tapes he had heard.

Jerry phoned Captain Fordham immediately. "Sid, I may have something more. Meet me at breakfast." Both team groups had breakfast (minus those on duty) at Hotel Zur Sonne, but at different tables. This morning, Jerry and Sid sat at a table for four on the opposite side of the dining room. Soon after they were seated, Rios and Chuck were invited to join them. All four then went through the continental breakfast buffet.

Jerry ate part of a sandwich he had constructed from his buffet selections. "I had a dream last night."

"Rios interrupted, "hope it was as good as mine," he chuckled.

"Quiet, deputy, this is an official report!" commanded Jerry, as he chewed the remnants of his sandwich. "When I woke up, I remembered someone on the tape mentioned a missing attorney; I can't remember the German word, but I think it meant attorney or lawyer. At any rate, the

Anwalt, that's the word, met with someone at our hotel. Last night Max and his wife were talking about a guest who didn't check out and left everything here."

"Outstanding!" exclaimed Sid. "That may put a whole new view on recent chatter. I'll be right back."

"Should we delay departure?" asked Major Rivera.

"Nope. I'll put someone one it. Be right back!"

Back home in Caribou, it was a time of silent alarms. The first was somewhat humorous. "Charlie Forty, Robert Twelve (a new reserve deputy, Attilio Bernardo, who was being trained by Deputy Roads). Silent alarm at Standard Oil station.

"SO, Forty, responding.

The alarm wasn't exactly silent. When the signal box the sheriff's department had installed was activated, an irritating sound transmitted over the sheriff department radio frequency. Every patrol unit could 'clearly' hear the signal. The department had several 'alarm boxes' loaned to businesses and residences that might be at risk for criminal activity. The dispatch office had a monitor to identify the unit transmitting. Patrol units had to suffer the sound until dispatch sent a deputy to shut off the alarm transmitter. The silent alarm wasn't silent to anyone with a radio.

Nobody at the alarm location could hear it. Therefore, it was a 'silent alarm'.

"I'm getting rather tired of this alarm. We have responded five times this week. The first four were false alarms. What do you want to bet this one is too?" complained Tillio.

Deputy Roads informed Deputy Bernardo, "The false alarms don't matter. Don't even think about false alarms. If you want to live to retirement age, you will treat every call as real and dangerous."

Tillio pulled Chris's Remington Model 870 police model shotgun from the center mount and said, "Yes, ma'am." Tillio handed Chris the weapon as they both exited the patrol car at the gas station. Several civilians were standing in the open service bay, staring at the blue and red flashing lights displayed on the sheriff's patrol car.

"Hands behind your head," Deputy Bernardo commanded.

Chris racked her shotgun (using the pump action to chamber a new round of ammunition). Tillio had already chambered a shotgun shell for Chris. The new deputy's 'help' created panic. When Deputy Roads pumped the slide on her shotgun, an unfired shotgun shell was ejected from her Remington and rolled across the concrete floor. Almost everyone simultaneously 'hit the dirt', well, in this case, hit the cement. Each was lying flat on the floor with hands behind their heads. Quick learners. Chris was trying not to laugh as she deemed the area secure.

Deputy Roads went into the back office and switched the alarm box power switch off. The alarm was silenced. "SO, Charlie Forty, code 4 (everything ok).

"Roger Charlie Forty," the dispatcher acknowledged.

After Chris located the station attendant, she inquired, "what's your problem?"

The cowed attendant responded, "I think you're the problem. Why are you pointing guns at my customers?"

"Because the alarm went off. Again." Chris retorted. "Any of those present might have been a criminal trying to rob you. Were you playing with the fob again?"

The 'fob' was a small device with a pushbutton on the surface to push in an emergency. The nervous attendant had depressed the button on all the prior alarms.

The shaken attendant replied, "well, maybe I pushed it by accident."

Chris directed Attilio Bernardo to get everyone up, check their identification, and release them.

"Charlie Forty, SO, status?"

"Forty, Ten-four. False alarm. I'm bringing the alarm box back to the office. Forty and Robert Twelve are back in service."

"You can't take the alarm," exclaimed the station attendant. "My boss won't be happy about this," the attendant whined.

"I'm not happy either. False alarms can get people hurt. This alarm is the fifth false alarm in less than a week. Give me the fob, and be happy that I'm not putting you in cuffs and taking you in."

The gadget was produced immediately. Attilio and Chris dismounted the alarm. Chris looked at her rookie and said, "you get to write this report, rookie."

"I will, Chris. Sorry. Thanks for helping me."

Chris looked away, smiled, and said nothing.

The second alarm wasn't even an alarm. The incident was evaluated much later. An earlier evaluation may have sounded an alarm. Alerts that weren't necessarily silent, can provide clues in investigators heads.

Chief Stands Tall Ferguson (Caribou Police Department chief of police) observed a person in a black car driving around the Grubb mansion, and shinning a car-mounted spotlight on the building. The car license plate was registered to Saul Bernstein. When Bernstein was stopped by Chief Ferguson, Saul explained he was with GSI, a private security firm, and was doing a security check for a client. Saul was released. The chief completed a comprehensive report that was filed with Caribou police department and Banner County sheriff department records. A copy was forwarded to the FBI in Cheyenne.

Jerry was pleased to be back in Caribou. Rios was happy to be home. Cheryl and Chris were delighted to have Jerry and Rios home. The bad news Molly had died was conveyed earlier. That left an empty spot in dispatch and the heart. Delta helped. He followed Jerry and Rios everywhere, tried to be close, and almost licked them to death. Jerry told Cheryl, "Delta missed us, but he goes home happily with Tom every night."

"He's like that with everyone he loves and trusts. You guys must be trustworthy. Hey, that might be a good campaign slogan."

"What campaign?"

"When you run for sheriff."

"No way. 'm happy."

"You might not be if someone besides Tom was sheriff. Shucks, you are a supervisor now. You may not even have a job under a new sheriff. A new sheriff might sell all your nice flying machines."

Cheryl gave Jerry a long kiss, and they adjourned to bed. Later Jerry gave a lot of thought to what Cheryl had said. "*Maybe,*" he thought as he drifted off to sleep."

Jerry woke refreshed, happy, and content. He thought to himself; *this last mission was the easiest he had ever performed for Burks. He summed up the assignment as Navy personnel in an Air Force facility, pretending to be in the Army, transported by an Army warrant officer in command of the overall mission. FUBAR from the start. However, the operation was successful, even with a Navy 0-6 (captain) pretending to be a warrant officer.*

Cheryl was happy to have Jerry home. She wasn't ever calm when she knew her husband was in a combat area. The medals and devices on his uniform were proof Jerry was a competent and courageous warrior, but those decorations were no guarantee he would come home safely in one piece every time. The Purple Hearts and wound scars were evidence Jerry wasn't bulletproof.

"Welcome home, Captain." Rios almost shouted. Lots going on since we got back."

Those who weren't aware Rios Rivera had been with Jerry, might be convinced Rios had been in Caribou.

"What did we miss?"

ELK HUNTING

Rios was visibly upset. "I have an elk license to fill."

Glenn pointed out, "you will still be here during hunting season."

"But I don't want to go. What will Chris do without me."

Tom pointed his finger at Rios and calmly reminded the agitated deputy, "Forty has done quite well during some of your other frequent duty absences."

"I haven't!" pouted Rivera. "You have other pilots to fly our aircraft."

"Yup, we do. Your wife is one of them," said Jerry. "I would send her, but she isn't an Army officer. You are the only deputy qualified to go to Army aviation flight school."

Rios knew he would attend Army flight training but pressed on. "Why does the sheriff's department need another helicopter pilot?"

Jerry's reply quickly answered that question, and simultaneously gave Rios new insight into the opportunity just handed to him. "It takes two pilots for the Jet Ranger to be flown safely. Only one pilot is needed to safely fly the Cessna. The sheriff's department has three fixed-wing pilots. We only have two rotary-wing pilots. Although one aviator can fly our Jet Ranger, two are needed for mission operations. We have two helicopter pilots. If one of those two is sick, or more likely, away on department duties or military activation, only one pilot is available. We can't justify owning and operating the Jet Ranger, the sheriff's office might lose operations money in our budget, and possibly even the aircraft. I can't let that happen. (Then the 'magic' words that made Rios sit up and take notice.) "Besides, it will mean a promotion and a pay raise for you. The department would have to hire someone else who is qualified if you don't take this opportunity. Then the department couldn't give you a raise or a promotion."

'Promotion' got Rivera's immediate attention. More money was a pleasant thought. "Promotion here (meaning the sheriff's department) or military (referring to the Wyoming Army National Guard where Rios was a reserve major)?"

"Both," Jerry informed Deputy Rios Rivera. "Promotion in the sheriff's department is guaranteed if you manage to graduate from rotary wing training. If Senator Burks can arrange for a National Guard major to get a flight school slot, I'm sure he can arrange for that major to get a silver oak leaf (the insignia that represents the rank of lieutenant colonel O-5 pay grade). Or maybe not, I don't know. When promotion boards are deciding which officers will get promoted, advanced training and expertise is often the deciding factor. Only a few get promoted to O-5 and up. If you can fly, it won't hold you back."

Rios looked at Sheriff Tom. Tom smiled and nodded his cowboy hat covered head. Rios was hooked.

"Now that we have someone to operate Jerry's big boy toys, can we move on to a more critical need?" interrupted Undersheriff Glenn Marvin. One of Glenn's responsibilities was the supervision of the department's dispatch center. "Molly will be hard to replace. We need to locate a suitable replacement and get him, or her hired, trained, and on the job."

Sheriff Flanigan addressed the entire group. "Any suggestions?"

No one spoke or even raised a hand.

'Ok, Glenn. Advertise the opening as 'entry-level dispatcher'," the sheriff ordered.

Jerry suggested, "why not announce two positions? Molly was the de-facto dispatch supervisor. Anyone interested could apply for either or both positions, including current dispatchers. That would be a promotion for someone already working for the department. Or we might attract a qualified outsider who might not apply for an entry-level position. Either way, we would get a qualified radio dispatch operator."

"Good idea, Jerry! exclaimed Undersheriff Marvin.

"I agree," Big Tom bellowed. "Go for it, Glenn. Nothing to lose. Might get lucky."

Jerry stood, slid his cowboy hat onto his head, and stated, "if that's all, Rios and I have elk calling our names."

"Have fun. Keep in touch."

"Will do, Sheriff. Come on, Rios, let's get out of here before someone wants to have another long, boring meeting."

"You have that almost right, Jerry. Someone may think of another 'opportunity' for one of us." Laughter followed Jerry and Rios out the door. Glenn and Tom were still laughing when the door clicked shut.

Willy J and Bob Weisberg had packed most of the necessary supplies and equipment in panniers. The panniers were carefully loaded and weighed. Strips of masking tape were stuck to the top flap with the weight marked on each with a marker pen. The pack horses could only carry a certain amount of weight, depending on the size of the horse. When the load was evenly distributed on both sides, the pack harness was less likely to shift and makes travel more pleasant for both horse and hunter.

"Great food," Willy J announced. "Pretty nice of your wives to get up early and cook for us."

Cheryl, Bonnie, and Chris, had surprised the lucky hunters with a huge breakfast. While their husbands were hunting, the ladies were going to Rapid City with plans to shop, visit a spa, and tour the casinos in Deadwood.

"Willy, you need a wife or at least a girlfriend," suggested Rios.

"Why? Yours take good care of me, and I don't have to finance their trip."

"Better be careful, Willy J. We all have guns," advised Bob.

"True, but I have the horses."

"Good point. Jerry laughed.

Cheerfully the hunters got horses caught; saddles and gear packed. Two large stock trailers accommodated the livestock, hay, and grain. Two quad-cab pickups were loaded with the remaining equipment, and the group began the drive to Saratoga, Wyoming. The plan was to spend the night at the Wolf Hotel and set up camp near French Creek campground early tomorrow. The horses had reservations for quarters in Saratoga too.

The Wolf is an old hotel, recently remodeled. It is comfortable and has good food. Orange, and military o.d. green camouflage, were the clothing color choices, as hunters flocked to the area for the opening day of hunting season. The Banner County contingent fit right in. They were seated at a table in the Wolf Hotel bar telling war stories over drinks. Famous Grouse if you must know.

"Jerry, what are you and your posse doing in Saratoga?" said one of two men in the bar not wearing orange clothing. he two were wearing county sheriff's uniforms, because they were the sheriff and undersheriff of Timber County.

"Willis how are you doing?" said Jerry, as he stood and shook the sheriff's hand. "We are hoping to help reduce your elk population."

"I heard tell there was a nice herd up high."

The two groups of law enforcement officers got introduced to each other. With shared interests, they were comfortable talking. The Timber County Sheriff was Willis Van Devanter.

"Are you related to Willis Van Devanter, the supreme court justice who was Wyoming's first and only United States Supreme Court Justice during the early 1900's," Willy inquired.

"Nope, no relationship at all."

Willis was in his second term of office. He and Jerry had met at the Wyoming Law Enforcement Academy while both were newly minted sheriff's deputies. Undersheriff Jacob (Jake) Bowman, was a former Wyoming highway patrolman.

Although the lawmen were very comfortable with each other, some of the bar patrons were uneasy. The Timber County sheriff and his undersheriff were wearing sidearms and had large five-point badges pinned to coats and shirts. As the customers began to discover there were six cops in the bar, some decided to seek a different location for their festivities. Jill Bascom, the bartender and night manager of the hotel, approached Willis. "Hi, Sheriff."

"Evening Ms. Bascom. Looks like a big crowd tonight."

"It sure is. The meeting room is vacant right now. If you and your group would like to move back there, I can get you fed before the kitchen gets overrun."

Willis turned to Jerry. "Jerry this is Jill Bascom. Jill, this is Jerry Burkley. He's a captain with Banner County sheriff's department." Willis grinned, "Jill is going to sneak us into the meeting room in the back and get us fed early if that will work for you guys."

Jerry took off his hat and said to Jill, "mighty nice of you, Ms. Bascom. Always nice to get moved to the head of the line."

Later Jerry mentioned to Willis, "the owner of a cop bar in Caribou, Desmond's Pizza, does the same thing."

"Which same thing?" Jake asked.

"Put the uniforms in the backroom, so the customers don't leave!"

"Works pretty well," commented Rios with a chuckle.

"Willis, you know this area. Where should we hunt?" inquired Bob Weisberg. "We thought going up from here would take us to a successful hunt area."

"It is a great area. Look at the orange around you in the bar area, and this is just one bar. Lots of hunters on this side. That also means a lot of congestion and competition for good camp locations."

"True," agreed Willy J.

"Your suggestions?" Jerry responded.

Van Devanter smiled, unbuttoned his right shirt pocket, and removed several business-sized cards. "Well, maybe this will help!" Willis, in the style of a card dealer, distributed four of the cards to Jerry, Willy J, Bob, and Rios. Embossed on the card was **'One entry to Elk Mountain Ranch-for access only. No Hunting'**. The card had an illegible signature. Willis went on to explain. "This card will give you access across the ranch to the Libby Flats area. That is where I would go hunting elk."

"That's what I said when Jerry and Rios were on their journey for the senator," reminded Bob.

"Why do we get this special treatment?" questioned Jerry.

"Several reasons." answered Willis. "I have the cards and permission to distribute as I see fit. The owner likes combat veterans and cops, so you guys are qualified. But mostly because I like and respect you. Banner County is a leader in Wyoming law enforcement. The four of you are leaders. Besides, I want to hunt Big Horn sheep."

Laughter broke out. The two departments developed a close bond of brotherhood then and there.

"Great meal, Bob," congratulated Willy J. Dr. Weisberg had cooked steaks to perfection, with fried potatoes and onions, over the fire pit.

Jerry added his praise as Rios said, "thanks."

"Quiet Judge. You get to cook tomorrow. Please do as well as Doc," commanded Jerry.

"Sure, Boss." Rios answered with a grin.

Rios River, the Judge, didn't intend to talk about Bill, the new K-9. It just slipped out. Seated around a fire, having a short after-dinner drink of Famous Grouse, had everyone relaxed.

"What is Tom going to do about a K-9, it appears Edna is in favor?" Bob Weisberg questioned.

Without hesitation, Rios volunteered, "that lady in Florida got us a young service dog in need of a new home. And, Louis, the guy I know in Mesa, is going to train Bill."

Rios was excited, and continued to spout. "Louis is going to move his dog training company to Caribou. Robinson Dog Training will be great for Banner County. Louis is a former Air Force K-9 handler. He would make a great reserve deputy." Just then, Rios realized he had 'let the cat out of the bag' about the dog. He shut up, looked at Jerry, and then down at the ground.

Jerry was aware of Edna's influence. Many of the deputies sometimes voiced the opinion that Edna ran the sheriff's department. They were only partly kidding. Edna's help and suggestions augmented Big Tom's leadership. Edna was the file that removed the rough edges. Edna made gentle suggestions. Tom listened. The department benefited.

Jerry was miffed he had not been kept in the loop, but he also realized the senator had deployed him for most of the period when decisions had to be made. Captain Burkley was also delighted his friends felt free to keep him informed.

"So, Judge, tell me about Bill. I assume Bill is a dog and not a deputy with special training needs." Jerry liked dogs. He was also comfortable with making Rios Rivera squirm.

The 'Law West of the Rio River', Judge Rios Rivera, was a deputy sheriff and an Army National Guard Medical Service Corps officer. Major Rivera was not, nor had he ever been, a judge. The title was a nickname bestowed upon him as a second lieutenant on active duty in Vietnam, by other Army soldiers when he skillfully resolved a tricky race relations problem early in his career. The name stuck. Rios was eager to tell Jerry all about Bill.

"After I mentioned to Edna I knew a dog trainer in Arizona; she suggested I call Louis. One thing led to another," muttered Rios.

"We can't hear you," Weisberg taunted.

"Speak up," ordered Jerry.

Rios sipped his Famous Grouse, looked at Willy, who had been uncharacteristically silent, and continued. "My friend Louis suggested I look at Delta's AKC (American Kennel Club) registration certificate for the breeder's name.

"And I would just bet Louis is the dog trainer," Jerry opined.

"Yes, Sir. Louis Robinson is a great dog trainer."

"And?"

"Delta's breeder's name was on the certificate, just as Louis suggested. Her name is Lisa Sloan. She operates Sloan's Lake Labradors in Jacksonville, Florida. There was a phone number too."

"So?" interogated Jerry.

"So, I called and told her what Edna wanted to know about an older dog. She was accommodating. Nice lady."

Jerry added ice to his Grouse and stared at Rios. Using his command voice, Jerry inquired, "Edna, and not the sheriff, set the parameters for your shaggy dog story?"

"Bill's not shaggy. He's a regal appearing Lab with short hair," Willy said, breaking his silence.

"Oh, oh." exclaimed Dr. W. He sat back in his chair, the front legs of the chair off the dirt. Bob just grinned as he watched 'round two'.

"And just how do you know how the dog looks, Willy? Are you involved with the Banner County Sheriff's Department expansion plans as well?"

"No, Boss. Although I do think a department K-9 is a good idea," Willy J volunteered.

"Well, I'm glad we all agree," Jerry pronounced.

Operation K-9 was discussed until all retired for the night.

The Banner County hunters were up and had horses saddled at dawn. Bob led the group to the edge of the Elk Mountain Ranch property. Willie swung his right leg smoothly over his horses' right hip and slid to the ground. He walked around to get the stiffness out and then grabbed his reins and the pack-saddle horse's lead rope.

Willy J tied his trail horse to the main fence post, opened the gate, and said, "come on through the gate. I'll close the gate and catch up/"

Willy J re-mounted his horse and trotted after the rest. Several miles of riding across national forest lands brought the Banner County group to the top of a vast mountain area.

"Wow," Rios exclaimed. "that's quite a view." The panorama of the desolate area called Libby Flats appeared cold and barren, even in the winter sunlight. Grey and white granite cliffs towered over the long valley along the east perimeter. Numerous snow-fed lakes, cascading streams, and snowbanks, dotted the landscape. Some areas were covered with grass, others with extended fields of granite rock. Lichen embroidered rock surfaces. The funny-looking trees with all the foliage only on the down-wind side made the scene appear alien.

The four riders felt like they were at the top of the world. The view was almost unlimited down long valleys. Steep mountainsides framed the valley sides. The rockslide areas made footing difficult for the horses.

"Listen to that wind. It sounds like it is moving through the trees towards us," shouted Doc to the group, his hand on top of his hat to keep it from blowing away.

"Yup," agreed Jerry. "even the tree-tops are moving in slow motion. Just think what those funny looking trees have to experience."

As they moved down the valley, elk sign was discovered. Not billboards, but rather the distinctive piles of digested food left where elk traveled. "Time to start walking," suggested Bob. "I think we found the elk herd."

Bob was correct. The hunters felt the adrenaline pump into their system as they tied the horses to scrubby trees, pulled rifles from scabbards, and moved on foot along the trail covered with elk tracks. Cresting a small hill, they saw elk. "Look at that!" Jerry pointed to hundreds of elk lying in the tree line, bedded down for the day. The hunters did what hunters do. Four elk were shot, almost simultaneously, and remained on the ground as the rest of the herd ran into the trees.

"Now, the work begins," commented Willy. The elk were carefully field dressed. The hunters began the process of loading elk onto their saddle horses. Leading the four horses on foot, Bob and Willy started back towards their camp with two of the elk carcasses. Rios and Jerry remained with the other two elk. The morning was warming up. Rios and Jerry laid in the sun talking while they waited for Bob and Willy to return with more horses. It was a glorious day for the successful hunting party.

SPOOKS, SPIES, AND OTHER THINGS

Willie, as usual, was complaining. "Harder getting the elk off the mountain, then it was to get everything ready, pack it all, and move everything to Bob's weird mountain top."

"True," said Rios. "Only Burks and Burkley provide such interesting challenges."

"Not so," argued Bob. "When we entered Libby Flats, we had no elk. Now we have four. Two of our elk have a nice set of horns to take home with us. And-"

"And what?" Jerry commanded.

"And, no one is shooting at us," Bob's remark brought general laughter.

"As Rios would say, true," Jerry replied. "at least not yet."

All four of the hunters had seen combat. Jerry's point was instantly made. Four tired hunters checked into the Wolf Hotel in Saratoga just before dark. The horses were fed, watered, and stabled for the night. Following much-needed showers, shaves, and a change of clothing, the Banner County deputies met in the Wolf Hotel bar. Willis Van Devanter, in civilian attire, greeted his brother law-enforcement friends. "My treat. We are going over to the Saratoga Inn across the river."

"Why not just eat here?" questioned Bob. "Nice place, good food and drinks."

"Saratoga Inn – nice place, good food and drinks also," replied Willis.

Jerry expressed the primary benefits of moving dinner down the road. "The Inn is quiet. We can visit and not be heard by others. Best of all, Willis is buying, even our drinks."

The sound of Banner County truck doors opening, then slamming shut, accented Jerry's persuasive argument.

Willy J was 'tail-end Charlie climbing into the front seat. "What's keeping you, Willy J?" asked Dr. Bob.

"That limo-like car over there. The gray one with DC (District of Columbia) license plates. "Looks like the cars our federal friends from the alphabet agencies might drive," Jerry commented.

"Maybe? But the guy who got out looks like the same fellow who glassed us (used field glasses to observe) while we were packing elk out of Libby Flats."

Willis volunteered, "I got the plate number. when we get to the Inn, I'll have my dispatcher run it." (Sheriff Van Devanter was referring to having the license plate number entered into the National Crime Information

Center system operated by the FBI. This computer system could identify vehicles and people wanted in connection with felony crimes).

Talk turned to elk hunting. The car and its driver were put on the back burner. The drinks and dinner at the Inn were outstanding.

A deputy from Willis's department delivered an envelope to Sheriff Van Devanter. Willis opened the envelope, glanced through the message sheet contents, and passed it to Jerry and Willy J.

```
                    NCIS
         SUBJECT INFORMATION FLAGGED=
         No Release without NTK ID#
         //SCREEN LOCKED//
         EOM
                    NCIS
         [NTK– Need to Know] [EOM – End of Message]
```

"Strange reply," observed Burkley. He passed the message to Willy and Bob. They quietly read the message form. The contents didn't take long to read. It was a short transmission. Rios looked over their shoulders and exploded, "that guy is a deep, dark, secret agent man."

"Even money," Willis agreed.

Jerry left the table and the speculation. Captain Burkley called Sheriff Tom at home, had Edna wake Big Tom, and when Tom answered the phone, brought him up to date.

"Tom, we need a different unmarked car down here yesterday." Jerry was frustrated." Get one of the new cars from McCall, if he has one available." His request was almost an order, not quite.

"Cash doesn't have any of the new cars in yet. The department has no spares."

Jerry again almost demanded, "see if McCall has a four-wheel-drive vehicle we can use."

The Grubb mansion had presumably been vacant for four years. Most people in Caribou, from the beginning, thought the building was empty. A few Caribou citizens weren't as sure. Part of the second group thought the former funeral home was haunted. Saul Bernstein encouraged residents to believe ghosts resided in the Grubb mansion.

Ghosts, ghouls, and other poltergeists, failed to deter Judge James Broderick, Banner County District Judge, from moving his unnecessary files into the old building. Carol and TG got the order. "Good location," exclaimed the Honorable James F. Broderick. "Get those boxes out of here. Start with those you stacked in my chambers."

"We are on it, Judge." TG and Carol were ecstatic, especially Carol. This assignment was almost over. Closing the lease arrangement had been frustrating. The title search, because of the many different owners, had been tedious. Finally, all the correct signatures were placed in the proper locations. Banner County had a ten-year renewable lease on the Grubb mansion. The Grubb mansion had a new sign identifying the building as the 'Grubb Annex-Banner County Courthouse'. Soon it simply became the 'Annex'.

Jerry wasn't happy. Acquisition of the Annex and his commitment to assist in moving files meant his house remodel, which was almost complete, might be delayed again. He grumbled to everyone, "Cheryl's going to kill me yet."

Cheryl thought it was funny. She loved to give Jerry the 'look' as she had fun exploring the 'spooky' annex.

<<< >>>

Sergeant Jack Falls supervised the off-duty deputies who had been conscripted (and paid overtime) for moving files. The boxes were heavy. Most were covered with years of dust. "Take a break," Sergeant Falls ordered. "Look around if you're so inclined. The truck with the next load of files won't return for an hour or so."

The deputies had carried boxes, one at a time, from the front entrance, up the front steps, and stacked in the front reception area. The files were always watched. Each box was then carried up a winding set of stairs and piled in the second-floor hallway. Finally, the file boxes were lugged down the hall and carried up a narrow stairway to the third floor. Willy J and his construction crew built and installed a shelving system in the spacious ballroom area on the third floor of the Grubb mansion before it began to be called the Annex.

Sweating deputies delivered files to their new home. Carol and TG pointed to the proper shelf location.

"It about time we got a break," complained one deputy. No one complained about being set free to explore the Annex.

"Look at that picture," Jack Falls exclaimed. "I think I saw the same one when I was in Cheyenne for the Story post."

"Think or know?" asked Willy.

"Pretty sure it's the same picture. That was a few weeks ago. The guy on the right side of the second row sure looks like the guy they autopsied."

Willy J was not a believer in coincidences. He called Jerry's cell phone number.

"Burkley. How is my remodel coming along?" Jerry had seen Willy's name on his caller ID.

"Still the same, Boss. I have some interesting information about the Cheyenne DB. Falls thinks Story's picture is on class photos hanging at the Annex and in the funeral home in Cheyenne."

"What kind of class?"

"The San Francisco College of Mortuary Science. It seems like that might be a small group. Maybe he was involved with the funeral home here," Willy speculated.

"Possible. Have someone visit with Bud Hayes. He appears to be the local ghoul expert."

Mr. Hayes would not have appreciated the title, but he had been with Mountain Shadows Funeral Home for many years. He was soon consulted by Lieutenant Schrader and Deputy Roads, who were acting as the lead detectives for a sheriff's department that had no detectives.

<<< >>>

"Don't you ever mention satin sheets to me again, ever!" Cheryl was very agitated. "I've spent hours trying to iron Bonnie's sheets, and they look as wrinkled as they did when I started."

Jerry and Cheryl were housesitting for the Weisberg's. Willy Harold was finishing the Burkley house remodel. The Burkley house was a mess. Doc needed someone to watch after his horses, two dogs, and a cat. Cheryl thought 'camping out' at the Weisberg residence was a good trade.

"Yup, I won't, but the satin sheets were fun to slide around on." Jerry avoided Cheryl's elbow to his ribs and smiled.

Doc and Bonnie smiled too when Cheryl apologized for not getting the sheets ironed adequately. "We never iron them, just plop them on the bed right out of the dryer," Bonnie chuckled.

<<< >>>

The Libby Flats board of directors met in emergency session. The subjects were events that troubled and worried the board. One of those concerns had previously been discussed. The other distressing situation was the presence of four Banner County sheriff's department deputies.

"The board will come to order," said President Richmond. Six of the eight members were present. Soon the board members were seated around a conference table with Dr. Fredrick Richmond. "Kalinda, please ask Mr. Bernstein to join us."

"Right away, Doctor," responded Kalinda Canton, the board secretary.

When Saul Bernstein entered the conference room, Dr. Richmond asked, "what does Global Security have for the board?"

Bernstein was the primary contact between GSI and the Libby Flats board of directors. "you have four Banner County deputies riding horses all over Libby Flats. They packed in across Elk Mountain and set up camp on the west side. They appear to be hunters, but as you know, few, if any, hunters enter the Flats from the northwest."

Delmar Bushmill raised his hand, and not waiting to be recognized by Richmond (a grievous violation of the authoritarian doctor's edicts), demanded "how do you know this?"

Fredrick Richmond ignored Delmar's breach of protocol. "Not only how, but why do you believe this board has any interest in Libby Flats, other than the foundation name. Or the Banner County cops for that matter?"

Saul leaned back in his chair, and entirely at ease, stunned the entire board. "GSI has sophisticated investigators and extensive monitoring capability. How I know the deputies are riding horses across Libby Flats is because I have observed them for several days. GSI is aware of your land near Libby Flats. GSI provides security for the Grubb mansion, which we have discovered Libby Flats Trust also owns, through a shell figure, who may also be related to one of your missing board members. GSI is curious why you purchased such odd properties as a vacant funeral home Would you like to enlighten me?"

George Smith quickly responded, "move to adjourn."

Jim Feltner instantly seconded the motion.

Saul was amazed to discover he was sitting alone at the table. The board members hurriedly departed, not only the room, but the town of Centennial. Emergency evacuations were part of the board's standing orders established by Dr. Richmond. The Libby Flats board could, and would, reconvene at another time and location.

MORTARY MEMORIES

Mr. Bud Hayes was a stately gentleman. His hair was white but neatly styled and combed. He wore a pin-stripe suit with a handkerchief in the breast-pocket which matched his dark red tie. He explained, "San Francisco College of Mortuary Science is a respected embalming school in San Francisco, California. Perhaps the best school of its sort in the United States. They have a president named Claude Grimm, and if that's not enough, a dean of students named Dale W. Sly. The humor is not lost on the students. The curriculum is twelve months in length and demanding. Graduates can work almost anywhere.

"Do you know or recognize anyone in this picture?" inquired Deputy Roads, handing Mr. Hayes the picture that had been found hanging in a basement room of the Annex.

"Of course, Mr. Palmer and Mr. Story both used to work for Mountain Shadows." Mr. Hayes pointed at two of the individuals in the picture.

<<< >>>

"Stands Tall Ferguson is the best law enforcement officer to send to San Francisco," Sheriff Tom Flannigan told Jerry Burkley.

"Why? I'm not arguing or doubting your judgment. I want to understand your reasoning."

"Tall has lived in Caribou his entire life. He is observant. His eyes and his past in Caribou will see a significantly different view of some situations that neither you nor any of our other deputies might discern."

"Will Stands Tall go? Will the tribal council let their chief of police investigate an off-reservation crime for us?"

Tom took off his cowboy hat, a rare occurrence unless a lady was present, and laid it crown-side down (as real cowboys guard their hats) on his desktop. Tom leaned back in his chair, put his boot-clad feet on the desk, and shut his eyes.

Jerry pushed Tom's boots off the desk. "Come on, enlighten me."

"Ok." Tom swung his boots back onto the desk. "Tall said he would go. The tribal council said Chief Ferguson could both help us, and take time off. Tall is the best for the assignment. Send Tosh (the county coroner and pathologist) with him. Then there will be two different opinions. Hank just got here."

A brief knock on the door was followed by Cash McCall storming into the sheriff's office. "When do I get that Blazer back? I'd like to have it back on the lot."

"Well, Cash," Jerry taunted the local, (and only) car dealer. "Rios is still looking for elk."

"The season is over." Cash fired back.

"Well, there is always next year. Hunters like to scout out the area."

Big Tom added his two cents. "When our new vehicles get here, maybe."

Jerry put a lid on the exchange. "Rios will be back tomorrow, Cash. Really, truly."

McCall left, and he didn't slam the door, which was a good sign.

"Tom," said Captain Burkley, "I think Tall and Hank will be a good team. Both will enjoy the Wharf, even if nothing is learned at the Sly-Grimm School."

The local newspaper provided information about the Libby Flatts Foundation Board and the board members. A public relations handout from the foundation took many words to say little.

CARIBOU BULLETIN

LIBBY FLATS FOUNDATION
BOARD OF DIRECTORS NAMED

The Libby Flats Foundation announced today the names and biographies of the board of directors selected at their last general board meeting. The foundation is a charitable organization involved in many local civic activities. The new board members are a diverse group which bring a wide range of experience and knowledge to assist in overseeing the various operations of the Libby Flats Foundation, according to their recent press release.

Dr. Fredrick Richards will continue as the President and Chairman of the Board for Libby Flats Foundation. Dr. Richards formed the foundation ten years ago and continues to guide Libby Flats into the future. Dr. Richards has degrees in political science and computer science. Dr. Richards helped designed the original Cray computer system.

Kalinda Canton serves as the Board Secretary. Kalinda has been with the foundation since its inception. Ms. Canton also serves on several other foundation boards.

Helen Palmer and her husband, Elmer Palmer, were invited to the board eight years ago when Dr. Richards expanded the foundation's involvement in Banner County.

Herman Story is a former National Intelligence Agency officer. Herman directed many computer information theft investigations.

James Feltner is a recent addition to the Libby Flats Board. Mr. Feltner is an internationally recognized computer expert. "I am happy to contribute to the Libby Flats Foundation mission."

Delmar Bushmill is a local rancher, with land holdings near Libby Flats and in Banner County near Caribou. This is Bushmill's first year on the Libby Flats board."

Lamar Robinson is a Banner County realtor. He is known for buying and selling ranch and farm estates.

Willy tossed the newspaper down on his desk. "This tells me nothing."

"Yup." Jerry and Tom agreed almost simultaneously."

"It tells me a lot," offered Chris. "Maybe because I've been working on both cases, but two of those board members have the same names as the DB's (dead bodies) in Cheyenne and Caribou."

"Good call," said Sheriff Tom Flannigan. "see if you can put faces to those two board members. All of them if you can."

"Ok, Jerry. Send both Rios and Chris. I guess we can save on the hotel expenses since married deputies can share the same room. Sheriff Tom and Jerry had been discussing witness/suspect interviews/interrogations of those who may have information about the Story body in Cheyenne and the Palmer body in Banner County.

"That's a fact, Sheriff. But, as I recall, we usually send two male deputies and have them share the same room."

"That was before we had a female deputy," retorted Sheriff Flanigan.

Jerry replied, "Forty (a nickname for Deputy Roads) is one of the lead deputies for Banner County in these two cases. I would call her a lead detective, but there are no detectives in this sheriff's department. She is a good investigator. Undersheriff Rios Rivera is also a good investigator.

Rios has the rank and experience to compel Laramie County to cooperate with Banner County."

"I agree. I just was interested in your justifications for sending them."

"Thanks, Boss," Jerry said, giving Tom a casual boy-scout style salute. "Who should we use for the two suspects in Banner County?"

"Have Lieutenant Pawlik make the assignments. We will be using deputies from his shift. Keep in mind; there are two others we will need to visit. Story's mother is a Libby Flats trustee. The ex-wife has Libby Flats shares. That might be a connection, or it may be nothing."

"Thanks, Sheriff. I'll put it in gear."

Lieutenant Pawlik passed the torch to Sergeant Brown, who in turn tasked Deputies Joe Chambers and Felix Johansen, possibly because they were C-25 and C-26 on the roster, to conduct the inquiry. The other shift deputies were pleased. None of them would have to do the long and often dull interviews. If the witnesses were hostile or possible defendants, it was an exasperating experience for the law enforcement officer. Driving around the county seeking bad guys was much better.

"Good duty, Chief. I think I could get used to this assignment!" Hank remarked. Dr. Henry Toshman, Banner County's new pathologist, and Stands Tall Ferguson, police chief of Caribou, Wyoming, had been recruited by the Banner County Sheriff's Department to check information about the two dead bodies. The task took them to San Francisco, California.

It was early evening, and the two were comfortably seated in the bar area of DiMaggio's Restaurant. Several friends in Caribou had suggested, no insisted, this was the place on the San Francisco Wharf for dinner. Their mission was to visit the San Francisco College of Mortuary Science and inquire about the persons in a picture that was apparently a class picture from the college. There was a print of the photograph in Cheyenne and Caribou. Information from the college might provide information.

Their hotel was a short walk to the college. Dinner was a taxi ride to the Wharf restaurant district. Dinner had been well worth the taxi expense.

"Yup, I must agree with you, Doc. My admiration for Jerry, which has always been great, just went to the top of the gauge. If we can garner some useful information tomorrow at that school, we will have a touchdown (it was football season).

"Or, we may have a fumble. Either way, we are having a fantastic vacation."

The next morning, Tall and Hank walked up the steep passage steps to the large white building at 1450 Post Street. The building was located at the peak of one of San Francisco's higher hills. The white building overlooked a small parking lot in front. Tall, wearing his police chief's dress uniform, rang the ornate doorbell.

The court records were old, the boxes dusty. The original glue for the labels had lost its grip, so to say. Tashana and Carol tried scotch tape but were dust defeated. The tape didn't stick to old labels and dusty boxes. Many labels had disintegrated over time.

Mr. Hayes climbed the narrow staircase and entered the ballroom that had once served as his casket showroom. A deputy stopped him. "I'm sorry, Sir. This is a restricted area. You will have to leave. How did you get here anyway? I know we secured the front entry and the back door before we brought files up here."

"I came in through the basement door," replied Bud Hayes.

Carol, overhearing the two voices echo in the large room, and seeing Mr. Hayes, intervened. "Is there a problem, Deputy Stephenson?"

"No, ma'am. I was just about to show our visitor out. He snuck in through the basement."

Mr. Hayes, with calm dignity, replied. "That is not accurate deputy. While I may have entered through the basement door, I did not sneak in. I used my key, as I have done for more years than you may be old." Bud turned to leave.

"Mr. Hayes, please stay." Carol requested. "Deputy, this is Mr. Hayes. He is working with Willy J, Judge Broderick, Captain Burkley, and me, to acquire this building. He is our expert. Mr. Hayes is cleared to move around the building as he wishes."

"Yes ma'am," acknowledged Deputy David Stephenson. "Sorry, Sir. I didn't know," Deputy Stephenson apologized to the stately gentleman.

"Mr. Hayes, do you know if there is any tape or adhesive anywhere in the building, or perhaps a good marker pen? We have a label problem." Carol explained their dilemma.

Bud took charge in a friendly, useful manner, just as he had provided for many grieving families during his career as a funeral director. I have materials to construct new labels and can mix a good glue paste that will hold, if my old supplies are still stored in the basement."

Mr. Hayes asked Carol and Tashana to collect damaged labels and write the necessary information for missing or incomplete tags on a yellow legal pad. He then told the ladies, "I'll go below decks (down to the basement) to set up a work desk." When Bud was in a cheerful mood, he frequently lapsed into Navy terminology, a left-over from several years of honorable service in the United States Navy. Words like 'bulkhead' (wall), 'line' (rope), and 'stand by to stand by' (wait), often crept into his conversation. He had often told apprentice embalmers to 'swab the deck' (mop the floor).

Bud carried a large bag of labels and the short notes created by Carol and Tashana down the narrow stairs. At the foot of the stairs, Bud set the container on the deck (floor). He opened a door on his right. The dark shaft disclosed no elevator. Bud released the brake but was unable to move the lift. *"Yup,"* Bud thought to himself. *"Someone locked the elevator on another level."*

Bud hauled the bag along the corridor and down the winding stairs to the lobby. The deputies would turn right and walk around to the basement stair entry outside the back door. Bud turned left, went past the porch door, and opened a door on his port (left) side. He descended another narrow staircase to the basement level.

"Well, I'll be darned. I have a new job. And right where I've spent most of my life. Wish Ruby was here to see it." Ruby was Bud's deceased wife.

Bud gathered an ink bottle, several nib pens, and a supply of the labels he formerly used to temporarily mark gravesites. Mr. Hayes removed his suit coat, shirt, and tie, hung them in a nearby closet, and in his tank top t-shirt, donned a transparent rubber apron (as he would have utilized for embalming) to protect his suit pants from stray ink drops. Mr. Hayes sat at his desk in the former employee lounge and began to make new labels. His calligraphy was remarkable. The new labels were impressive.

Bud Hayes was carefully lettering labels when he heard footsteps on the inside stairs. The heavy clomp of boots preceded the entrance of three deputy sheriffs. Bud knew they were most likely assigned to the records detail. T-shirts with Banner County sheriff screen prints, jeans, a belt with both a badge holder and a holstered service weapon, served as identification. Bud had seen them moving file boxes to the third floor but didn't know them.

"Welcome." Bud greeted. "Anything I can do for you?"

"No, Sir. We are on a break and just looking around," offered Dan Taylor.

These two guys are Ira Wheaton and Ivan Morton. We are all deputies and today's slave labor."

Bud countered, "I was under the impression you were paid volunteers. I also heard you enjoyed working with the two ladies. Am I wrong?"

"No, Mr. Hayes. That is correct. I was joking."

"And gripping," Deputy Morton observed.

"Ok, true story. Hey, Mr. Hayes, is this place actually haunted?"

Bud laid his nib pen carefully on a folded pile of kleenex, leaned back in his office chair, and placed his polished oxfords on the desk. "Only in my memories," he replied.

"What does that mean?" inquired Ira Wheaton.

"Well, twenty or thirty years ago, kids were living here. The oldest was fun to have around. At first, the tyke was just a little kid with an inquiring mind. See those plugs near the floor over there?"

"Yes, Sir, I do," answered Ira. "They are kind of funny looking."

"Funny plugs usually look funny. When the Grubb mansion, this building, was constructed, no electricity was available. Later cross-shaped little posts with cloth-covered wire were placed inside the walls to provide electric lights. When new electric wires replaced cloth, the wall plugs remained. You can put in a light bulb or a screw-in adapter for connecting cords. The adapters can be unscrewed and removed; a light socket remains. Young Master Barton Laramore would crawl over to an outlet,

131

unscrew the adapter, and stick fingers into the socket. Bart was fortunate not to be electrocuted."

"Cute," said Ira Wheaton.

"Doesn't sound haunted to me," added Taylor.

"Well," Mr. Hayes began another story, "maybe this is more on point. Young Master Laramore had a crib in that little room across from the elevator on the second floor."

"What elevator?" exclaimed Dan Taylor.

SMALL SECRETS DISCLOSED

The portly man opened the big door and gruffly told Tall and Hank, "new students enter the classroom door over there." The man at the door was wearing a white jacket similar to those worn by hospital doctors. His plastic nametag wasn't much help

MAC
EMBALMING PROFESSOR
San Francisco College of
Mortuary Science

Hank stuck out his hand and exclaimed, "Mac, good to see you again. Dale or Claude here today?"

Mac McGonigal might look slow, but he was confident he didn't know either of the strangers. "Only by appointment. Since you obviously are not students, I will need to see some identification. Then you can tell me your interest in President Grimm and Dean Sly One of you is dressed as a cop so I would like to see some official credentials, not driver's licenses."

One of the reasons Mac was well-liked by his students was Mac's ability to cut through BS and see events clearly.

Hank and Tall handed Mac their newly issued Banner County Sheriff's Department badges and I.D. cards they carried in new leather folders. Mac observed the shiny badge case and was about to send them away when Chief of Police Ferguson also handed Mac his well-worn Caribou Police Department badge case.

"Professor," Stands Tall advised Mac, "Dr. Toshman sometimes gets ahead of himself. Hank is a pathologist. I'm sure you know how they get with live people."

Mac grinned, his large mustache accenting the smile.

Chief Ferguson continued, "we are both from Banner County, Wyoming. Our sheriff, Tom Flannigan, sent us to you. Tom hopes you may have information about two of your former students. Both are persons of interest in two murders in Wyoming, which may be connected."

Tall's speech was the most Hank heard uttered by Chief Ferguson at one time. Mac had listened carefully and was now inclined to assist. Mac escorted Tall and Hank to his sparse office next to a large embalming classroom. The professor dispatched a student to the records office for the available information. Soon the two deputies concluded the trip to San Francisco would not produce essential details. The names were on the pictures of the two men. The school files had nothing they didn't already know.

"No feathers in our cap," remarked Tall, "but a nice assignment."

The two deputies were halfway through a commercial airline flight to Denver. "Yup, as Jerry would probably grunt. I wish we had more, Hank took a sip of his overpriced drink and said, "may we have such a good working vacation again."

Tall took a swallow of his beer. "Yup!"

<<< >>>

Dr. Toshman and Chief Ferguson were content and happy with their investigation. Two other teams were learning a lot about nothing as well, and their details were not a vacation.

Rios Rivera was not a happy camper; his deployment to flight school was not a vacation. Rios was on extended active duty as a Wyoming National Guard major. Rios had been 'volunteered' by Jerry Burkley to undergo rotary wing flight training at Fort Rucker, Alabama. Major Rivera was the senior ranking student leaning the complexities of helicopter flight. Many pilots, especially fixed-wing aviators, joked the helicopter wasn't entirely invented. Others observed helicopter flight was not possible. Helicopter blades just beat the air into submission. Rios often thought to himself, *"I'm getting too old for this crap."*

The weather was hot and humid. More insects were flying than the host of choppers at Rucker. Bugs irritated Judge Rios in Vietnam, and they still did. Right now, he had one major complaint. As the senior Army officer student, Rios was also the student company commander. That entailed a lot of extra work and forced him to give up either sleep of study time. Flying the Huey wasn't as tricky as flight theory. Major Rivera needed time to study theory.

Judge Rios, his old Vietnam nickname, was frequently used by old friends. When the other students learned of this appellation, it got used — a lot.

One benefit, or detriment, given the senior student officer, was a private telephone in his room. "Hey, Judge." Rios heard when he answered the incessant ringing.

"What do you want?" was the short query. The caller was Jerry Burkley.

"Sheriff Flannigan wants you to take care of your dog."

"What are you talking about?"

"You, and others, found not only a dog trainer but also a dog. Thanks to you, Banner County now must hire a K-9 officer. I should take it out of your raise."

"What raise?" More money was news to Rios.

"For passing rotary wing training and being the qualified deputy that Sheriff Tom is going to hire the day after you finish your active duty commitment."

"What commitment"? I'm just tdy (temporary duty)."

"Not a 'major' deal for a lieutenant colonel selectee. The senator (John Burks) says you need six more weeks of 'real flying'. First, though, you must fly to Jacksonville, Florida, and check out the dog."

Rios thought – *"What?"* and was about to voice much more when Sheriff Tom entered the conversation.

"Rios Rivera – you have successfully completed rotary wing flight training at Fort Rucker. Burks procured a promotion to 0-5 (lieutenant colonel) for you. You are a 'selectee' on the promotion list. Your flight familiarization assignment for six weeks will be at Fort Carson, Colorado. You have four days delay in reporting to Carson. You can check out our new K-9. He is a Lab, and his name is Bill."

Willie J then chimed in. "You are going to Sloan's Island Labradors in Jacksonville, Florida. The breeder's name is Lisa Sloan. Bill is a three-year-old service dog. is service person-handler died. Bill is available to be retrained."

Rivera was overwhelmed. The information was too much to compute. "What?" That was all he could get out.

Jerry continued the information narrative. "Get packed. The school will pin wings on you at morning formation. Your buddy, Louis Robinson, will meet you after the ceremony, and I'll fly us to Jacksonville." Rios was speechless as the phone clicked, and the dial tone resumed. Major Rivera's fellow students were surprised. Some were outraged.

"How come the major gets special treatment?"

"Do we get to graduate early?"

"Hell, he even gets a cake assignment."

Colonel Swartz, the student battalion commander, firmly stated, "order in the ranks. Field grade officers are entitled to expedited training whenever possible." [Majors, lieutenant colonels, and colonels are field grade officers. Lieutenants and captains are referred to as company grade officers. Generals are flag officers.]

Major Rivera has been selected for promotion to lieutenant colonel, and his expertise is needed elsewhere," Colonel Swartz informed the student pilots.

"Yup," Jerry smiled. *"to clean up after a big dog,"* he thought to himself.

<<< >>>

Louis Robinson established his dog training center in Caribou, Wyoming.

The Caribou Bulletin wrote:

MAKE YOUR DOG YOURS

Robinson Dog Training (RTD) Is now open in Caribou. Louis is a former Air Force dog handler. RTD is a certified dog training facility. Louis is a member of the Banner County Sheriff's Department reserve. As a reserve deputy sheriff, Louis is a fully qualified law enforcement officer. He also serves as the department's K-9 training officer.

Banner County Sheriff ,Tom Flannigan, informed our reporter that the newly formed K-9 (canine or dog) division is a new program. "We have two dogs. One is a retired service dog, who was the loyal companion and mobility dog for Molly Cook. Molly was a long-time dispatcher. Everyone in Caribou and Banner County depended upon Molly. Her dog, Delta, still presides over dispatch and the rest of the department as well," Big Tom told our reporter, "several officers suggested a K-9 division be formed since the department had inherited a dog. One thing led to another. Louis will supervise and train our new dog and Delta.

The new police dog's name is Bill. The name is a memorial to a Vietnam veteran, William Jones. Warrant Officer Jones is the recipient of The Medal of Honor. Several of the Banner County sheriff's deputies, including Captain Jerry Burkley, served with Mr. Jones in Vietnam.

Jerry handed Rios a copy of the newspaper article. "Now it's up to you, my friend."

With a quick step, and happy to be back working as a deputy sheriff, rather than being an aviation student, Judge Rios grabbed his bags and stowed them in the familiar Cessna 206. His enthusiasm dimmed when he realized Jerry was sitting in the right (fixed-wing instructor seat) and Louis, with gear, was in the back seat.

"I think Jerry expects me to fly this thing. I just learned to fly rotary wing, and he thinks I can fly a fixed-wing airplane. No! NO!"

Of course, Captain Burkley did expect precisely that. "Preflight is complete, Major, Sir. You can crank up at your leisure Or in the next couple of minutes. If not, you will have to go to OPS (Operations) and file a new instrument flight plan."

Louis was having a hard time trying not to laugh out loud.

Rios had been *"HAD"*.

Rios, after a short wait, while he thought it over, climbed into the left seat and started the checklist. Jerry gave the appropriate responses. With some assistance from the IP (Instructor Pilot) in the right position, Rios taxied to the active runway. That procedure, Rivera discovered, was more straightforward than putting a helicopter into a ground hover and then lifting off. *"They were right. Helicopters are not fully invented yet,"* Rios thought.

DOGS AND LITTLE GIRLS HAVE SECRETS

Sloan's Island Labradors was a smooth, well-run operation. Lisa Sloan, the dog breeder, was a charming lady who loved and cared about the puppies she brought into the world. She and Louis were immediate friends.

Just as Rios Rivera was feeling like a 'fifth wheel'. Lisa turned to him and said, "thank you for bringing us all together. You are creating a new life and career for a loyal service dog. Bill will serve and protect you with honor."

Rios turned to glare at Jerry. "What should I know that everyone here seems to have been told?"

Louis casually remarked, "I'll bet he didn't read the memo you sent."

"He must not have read it. He has been sort of preoccupied." Jerry asked Rios, "did you read the memo?"

"I wasn't preoccupied, I was learning to fly. What memo?"

"Probably the one that the sheriff posted on the bulletin board announcing that I was a certified reserve deputy and the K-9 trainer for the department," Louis announced.

"What else?" demanded Deputy Rivera.

Jerry joined in. "Wasn't that the same memo that named the new K-9 officer and the commander of the K-9 division?"

"I think it may have been the same one," Louis replied.

Lisa started to giggle. "Oh. You poor boy."

Dead silence filled the room. Then Rios exploded. "Why me? What will Chris say?" Then Rios stormed around the room. "First, you make me go to flight training that I didn't want to do. Now you want me to be a dog-sitter. I don't want to do that either."

Lisa jumped in on the so-far one-sided discussion. "Deputy, you are gaining a partner who could save your life. You won't be dog-sitting. More likely, Bill will be deputy-sitting."

"Couldn't have said it better, Mrs. Sloan, said Louis.

Jerry calmed the waters. "Judge, this is the promotion Sheriff Tom promised. You will be one of three division commanders. I have patrol, Joe Chambers has detention, and you have K-9. As for Chris's reaction, she suggested it to Tom.

Rios was quickly calming down. "You and Chambers are both captains - - - "

142

"Yes, Captain Rivera, you are. Would you now like to meet Bill?" suggested Jerry.

The smile on the new K-9 division commander's face was brilliant. He hugged Lisa and just said, "thanks."

Lisa took Rios's hand and led him to a small enclosure to meet his new working partner.

Brynna picked the cozy little room at the end of the second-floor corridor across from the ancient elevator to spend the night. She was the only person in the old mansion. Others had been entering and leaving for the last week. Brynna had been living in the deserted building for over a month. Except for the previous week, no one had entered.

"This is a nice room. And I can hide in the closets on the wall. Let's see, there are four big closets. I think I can always hide in one of the drawers too," Brynna thought. *"Tomorrow, I think I will explore the basement."* Brynna wrapped the old blanket around her thin, pre-teen body and immediately went to sleep.

The next morning the sun woke Brynna from her slumbers. She stored her blanket in one of the drawers. Brynna dressed in clean clothes and rode the antique elevator down one and a half floors.

"I think I've got this thing solved. Pull the rope that sets the brake against the big wheel thing, so I can pull that round metal thing out of the

post. Then, let's see, oh yeah, pull the brake rope the other way so that this platform can go up and down. Now, I remember. Pull the thick rope on this side, and that big wheel turns and lowers, the other big rope pulls it up."

Brynna slid the metal pin out, jerked the thin brake line, and used the big rope to lower the old elevator slowly. When she reached the first floor, she slowed the decent with the wheel rope, and with the brake rope she got the elevator stopped at ground level.

"Cool, here we are. Breakfast, then explore." Brynna rewarded herself.

Brynna fiddled with the door window and crawled through. A short walk allowed Brynna to blend in with a family attending a Salvation Army breakfast. She ate heartily and returned to the Grubb mansion Brynna re-entered through the window but used the elevator to continue down. She locked the elevator at the basement level. No one could use the old elevator with the locking pin inserted, unless they were in the cellar.   *"This is scary, but fun too. I wonder what's down here. Those guys hauling boxes upstairs weren't down here long."*

The youngster wandered around. There wasn't much to see. Exploring, though, has its rewards.

"Neat. Stairs going up. I won't have to use that old elevator. Well, I want to go to the other end first."

Brynna did. The furnace, which wasn't working, an area that looked like a tool storage room or workshop, and some storage cupboards, were all she first observed.

"Interesting. A lot of daylight coming through the wall. I think something might be there for me to investigate. Oh, lookie, lookie. I do believe I have found another door."

And she had. Brynna pulled herself over a short wall onto a flat area before the door. There was, indeed, a door. Brynna managed to pull the panel open. Inside was a large area beneath the mansion.

Brynna looked around. She was excited. *"Wow. Dirt back here. A cement wall over there."*

Brynna was looking at a long hallway entirely constructed, top-bottom-sides, of concrete. It looked like a tunnel to somewhere.

<<< >>>

"Jerry, Senator Burks on three," said the voice on the intercom.

"Thanks," Captain Burkley replied as he pushed button #3 on his phone.

"Morning, Sir. Are we going on your campaign trail?" 'We' was Jerry, Willy J, Bob Schrader, and Mrs. Rose Burks, the senator's wife.

"That's the plan. I understand the Cessna 414 the campaign leased will carry eight; two pilots and six passengers, baggage and fuel. Is that correct?"

"Yes, Sir."

"Good, I have one more passenger."

"No problem, Sir. Make him pack light. There are no problems with the flight itinerary."

"Then, Mr. Burkley (referring to Jerry's military rank/title), please ask Cheryl to join us."

"My pleasure, Sir. May I tell her why?"

"Certainly. I believe my recommendation for Banner County sheriff may carry more force if both you and Cheryl appear with me at the podium. Especially if you have already given a speech recommending me to be your next president."

"I can only reply. Yes, Sir, and do my best to comply with my orders."

John Burks laughed. "Jerry, you haven't changed a bit since I met you at Rucker. Thanks for the memory, as Bob Hope would say. File for sheriff. Tom agrees. Keep your mouth shut in public and put together a good campaign committee. I'll see you in Paul's Valley Friday." Pauls Valley, Oklahoma, was Senator Burk's residence.

The phone line went off before an astonished Jerry Burkley could say, yes, Sir.

Fort Carson, Colorado, sits below the towering mountains to the west, at 6,000 feet. That is several thousand feet higher in elevation than Fort Rucker. At this altitude, pilots have many flying adjustments to make before and after take-off. High temperatures combined with high altitude lower the performance characteristics of aircraft. One instructor told his students, "High altitude and low power kill!

The Blackhawk UH-60 helicopters flown by the pilots into and out of Butts Army Airfield experienced this unique challenge daily. Major (LTC selectee) Rios Rivera incurred two additional problems.

ORDERS EXTRACT
FORT CARSON, COLORADO

Rivera, Rios NMI, MAJ, WYARNG: Assigned10SFG Flight Training Section for UH-60 transition/qualification. Fort Carson, Colorado Springs, Colorado.

Rivera, Rios NMI, MAJ, WYANG promoted lieutenant colonel, USAR. DOR concurrent with United States Senate concurrence.

Upon certification-qualification: subject officer released from active duty; assigned WYARNG, 1022nd Med Detachment, Cheyenne, WY; w/duty as rotary wing aviator, HU-1D and UH-60 helicopter.

[note to the reader; DOR is date of rank. Promotion to lieutenant colonel and higher rank requires U.S Senate approval.]

LTC (lieutenant colonel) Rivera transitioned into the Blackhawk. In the process, he learned the intricacies of the armed helicopter and the aggravations of high altitude. It was a significant change from Rucker, but made Colonel Rivera a competent, professional aviator.

Upon his discharge, Rios believed he would have to suffer the indignities of catching a ride to the civilian side of Butts Army Airfield and fly an airline to Cheyenne. He was unaware of other means of transport to Caribou. LTC Rivera was double, maybe triple pleased, and amazed to discover his wife and the Banner County Cessna were waiting for him on the departure ramp. [The reunion between husband and wife was warm and tender.]

Rios was disgusted to learn he had arrived just in time for his monthly UTA (unit training assembly or 'drill weekend') After much public display of affection on the ramp at 1022ⁿᵈ Med Det, Chris flew back to Caribou and Rios donned his green bag (nomex flight suit).

"Sheriff Tom, Les Boden is on line three for you," announced Big Tom's secretary, Sara Alzate. Les Boden was the sheriff of Canyon County, Wyoming. "Morning, Les. What can I do for you this beautiful morning?"

"Hi, Tom. It could be a better morning, I guess. Salt Lake Center (A Federal Aviation Administration flight operations center) reports a single-engine plane dropped off the radar in the southern part of Canyon County. An airline cargo plane sent a PIREP (pilot report) of a faint elt (emergency location transmitter) signal somewhere between you and me."

How can I help?" Tom replied.

"You have airplanes, and I don't. Could you use one of your guys to conduct an air-search of the general area?" requested Les.

" You bet. Don't be surprised by my guy. Sounds like a girl. Of course, that may be due to the fact my guy is a girl," chuckled Tom.

Les laughed as well. "I heard you had a female deputy. I take your warning to mean she is also a pilot." It was a statement, rather than a question.

"She is. We call her Forty most of the time, but her name is Chris. She was a little miffed when Jerry and her lieutenant let her think she failed qualifications. Chris is Charlie Forty and a good deputy, as well as a good pilot. I'll have her call you for details. I will put our Cessna 206 into search and rescue status. You can use the mutual aid radio frequency to contact Three-Three-Sierra-Delta when the plane is in the area."

"Thanks, Tom. I'll keep you informed."

Dispatch informed Chris of her assignment. "Charlie Forty, Sierra Delta"

Chris pulled the microphone from the dash holder and responded. "Charlie Forty, go ahead."

"Charlie Forty, assist Canyon County with a search for a possible aircraft crash. Contact Two-Six-Charlie-One on mutual aid once you are airborne. Canyon County SO will provide further information."

"Copy Sierra Delta." Chris hung her Motorola microphone back on the hook in her patrol car, made a u-turn and started towards Caribou Airfield where the Banner County Sheriff's Department Cessna 206 was hangered.

She resisted the urge to activate her overhead red and blue lights and use the siren. Chris understood time was not a significant factor.

"Charlie Forty, Charlie Twenty-five (Deputy Felix Johansen). I have Cecil with me. Do you want me to pick you up?" Cecil Atwell was a Banner County reserve deputy (Robert Three) and a fixed-wing pilot. "Sheriff Tom thought I could be an observer, and you and Cecil could handle the flight."

"Works for me. I'm close to the office. I'll meet you there."

"Copy Forty."

Chris through to herself. *"That will work well. Two observers can look, and I can fly. And two big guys can push the 206 out of the hangar."*

The two big guys did indeed push the Cessna out of the hangar while Chris talked to Sheriff Boden on the phone.

"Chris, I have a report from Salt Lake Center that a single-engine Piper Cherokee disappeared from the center radar screen about the county line," Sheriff Bowden began Deputy Roads' briefing. "The plane is a four-place civilian aircraft with three souls on board. (three people). The good news for searchers is that the Cherokee is red with white trim, which should make it easier to see against snow or foliage."

"Yes, Sir." replied Chris. What are the coordinates?"

Sheriff Boden gave her that information and continued, "the three onboard are a mother, father, and their ten-year-old daughter. Look hard."

"We will, Sheriff."

Chris and Cecil completed the pre-flight inspection of the Cessna 206. The three deputies climbed into the plane and fastened seat belts. Cecil read the checklist as Chris moved switches and checked instrument indications. Both pilots indicated to each other they were satisfied the aircraft was ready to fly. Chris yelled "clear" out her side window and started the engine. When the props were spinning, and the engine sounded smooth, Chris began to taxi. Soon the plane was moving from the hangar to the active runway.

"Aircraft in the vicinity of Caribou Airfield, Cessna Three-Three-Sierra-Delta, taxi from hanger to active runway Two-Six." This announcement warned other aircraft in the Caribou area of the Cessna's movement. There was no control tower at Caribou Airfield. Pilots informed each other by radio to avoid conflicts.

Chris pushed the throttle handle forward, and as the plane gained speed down the runway, she eased the wheel back. Sierra Delta lifted gently into the sky. As the Cessna gained altitude, Chris retracted the flaps she had used on takeoff, adjusted the engine RPM, and eased into a climbing right turn to put her search team into the suspected crash area.

SNOW SECRETS

Sheriff Flanigan asked his secretary, "Sara, would you please have all supervisors, sergeants, lieutenants, captains, and the undersheriff, meet with me in the conference room in an hour?"

"Sure. Are we expanding the search?"

Sara Alzade had been Sheriff Tom's secretary and sometimes dispatcher for many years. Tom often thought Sara knew what he was going to do before he did.

"Planes are hard to find. If it did crash and we locate it, the NTSB (National Transportation Safety Board) and the FAA (Federal Aviation Administration) investigators will want the area secured. We will be expected to support the agencies, and we will assist in any way we can."

"I thought you hated the feds, Sheriff."

"I do. But it is my job to assist when it helps the public."

Sara nodded her head in agreement. "At least I get to wake up some supervisors."

Sara was broadly smiling as she left Tom's office. The first supervisor she would call was the patrol supervisor, Captain Jerry Burkley. Jerry had just worked the midnight shift and was probably now sleeping like a baby. Sara was sure she could persuade Cheryl to hang up the phone and let Jerry's phone ring until he answered. Sara was correct. She heard Cheryl giggle as she hung up.

"What do you want?" said a grumpy chief of patrol.

"Hi, Jerry. Sara Alzade calling for the sheriff. He wants all supervisors to meet in the conference room at ten."

"Then let me finish my eight hours."

"Ten this morning, not tonight, Captain. You have less than an hour."

"Crap, ok, on the way. What's the urgency?"

Sara let up, but just a little bit. "We are assisting Canyon County to search for a presumed airplane crash site."

"I'll go to the airport then." Said Jerry as he started computing search scenarios."

"Forty, Robert Three, and Charlie Two Six, are already airborne in Sierra Delta. I think the sheriff may be planning on a long ride through the woods. Got more calls to make."

Jerry was not a happy camper, he was tired, and would prefer flying to riding a horse. He also knew horses were better than a long walk in the woods. Jerry had made some of those long walks in the jungles of Vietnam and other locations John Burks had arranged.

The conference room was crowded, more than crowded. Besides the sheriff and Undersheriff Glen Marvin, three captains, three lieutenants, three sergeants, and the reserve chief, was the Caribou chief of police, and a few administrative clerks and off-duty dispatchers, who had smelled the coffee, and noticed the open donut boxes.

"Is there anyone still on patrol?" Jerry asked Joe Pawlik.

"Sure, Cap. I think Chambers and what's his name, the reserve deputy with the Italian name - - -."

"You mean Attilio Bernardo, the pawn shop owner?"

"Yup, that's the guy. He and Charlie Two-Nine are going into Caribou to capture some more donuts. If they see a robbery in progress or a morning DUI, I'm sure they will inquire."

"Joe, that is not doing our job." Jerry was getting agitated.

"Relax buddy. I'm just bustin your chops. All day and swing shift deputies are on the street, except for the supervisors and the donut detail."

"Joe, I think I may keep you on the payroll, despite my recent doubts."

Both were still laughing when the donut detail returned. Jerry grabbed two caramel covered long johns, several napkins, and sat in the office chair reserved for the patrol supervisor.

"Ok, Sheriff, you can start now." Jerry's announcement generated chuckles and a few outright laughs.

"Sit down," Sheriff Tom commanded. All present knew the sheriff was concerned. His bushy mustache neither pointed up, a good sign nor down, an ominous look. The grey 'stache' and the sheriff's mouth were flat.

"We are assisting Canyon County in a search for an aircraft crash. Salt Lake Center lost radar contact in the forest service area that borders Canyon and Banner Counties. Salt Lake Center called Canyon County, and Les Bowden called me. Our Cessna is deployed with two deputies and a reserve deputy. Bowden has a horse unit deployed from the north. We will do the same from the south.

Captain Burkley raised his hand. Big Tom acknowledged Jerry and took a big bite out of the sugar covered donut Sara had carefully put on the podium for him

"Tom, do you want the Jet Ranger deployed as well?"

Tom swallowed some donut and chased it with some lukewarm coffee from his mug.

"Let's keep it in reserve until we know more. Three people are traveling on that plane. One is a little girl." Many were aware Tom and his wife, Edna, had lost their only child when she was nine.

"The plane is a four-place single-engine Piper Cherokee, the low wing version. It is red. That might help if it is out in the open. In thick trees or plowed into the snow, probably not. Jerry, set up a ride. Carl Tafoya is bringing in his horses and has tack assembled. I want a command center here, and a horse, car, or aircraft mobile command center ready."

Other assignments followed. The meeting quickly broke up The office staff and off-duty dispatchers devoured the remaining donuts.

Jerry assigned Lieutenant Joe Pawlik, Reserve Lieutenant Willy Harold, Dr. Weisberg, and Captain Joe Chambers to his search team. Captain Burkley correctly assumed Carl Tafoya would join them, both from a sense of duty and to watch over his string of horses. Jerry had worked with and along-side all these men. They were experienced horseback riders and familiar with the mountain area they would be searching. As the author, Louis L'Amour, often described the heroes in his books, "these were men with sand you could ride the river with." (or something like that.) Good men to have by your side."

The possible confusion of having two riders named 'Joe' was addressed by Jerry during his briefing to the deputies on the way to Carl's ranch. Jerry concluded by stating, "use a first or last name while we are riding, except for our two Joes. Pawlik is "L-T" (military slang for lieutenant). Use call signs over the radio. Any questions?"

"Has Forty observed anything helpful yet?" asked L-T.

"No. You will probably hear anything as soon as I do. She is using the mutual aid channel to communicate."

Joe Chambers inquired. "If someone locates the plane, do we still make this ride?" Jerry grinned. He knew Joe could use the overtime pay if the search, or this trail ride extended. "That will depend on what we find and where. The desired response would be helicopter extraction. Sheriff Tom has asked the Wyoming Adjutant General for support, and we have the Jet Ranger. Since I am here, and Rios is in Cheyenne, there is only one pilot available for the Ranger. I don't wish to have my bird bent. Our chopper won't be used, except for an emergency."

Lieutenant Pawlik added, "our team, or Sheriff Bowden's search team, or both, will be used to assist the pilots so they don't have to get out of the aircraft. Hard to leave a whirly-bird in park or idle with no pilots if they have to park on the side of the mountain."

Carl had eight horses, six saddled and two pack horses loaded.

"Hey, Carl, great job." advised Jerry.

"No sweat. Sheriff Tom gave me a list. I think I have everything we need. Let's get everyone mounted up."

"Colonel Rivera, your superb flying skills have been requested. If you wouldn't mind, sir, the major would like to see you in his office, full flight gear."

The bearer of this news bulletin was SPC5 Ronald Wing. Wing was a 1022nd Med Det (WYARNG) flight medic. The 'major' was the operations office. Technically, Rios was the 1022nd commander. However, LTC Rivera was still in transition training in the UH-60 Blackhawk helicopter used for medivacs by the unit. Wing took joy in baiting the new lieutenant colonel. Both men had worked a special operation mission with Warrant Officer Burkley and were good friends.

Rank was not always a factor in the national guard where an employee in a civilian job may be a military commander and his boss a subordinate on guard weekends or at annual training sessions.

"OK, Ron, what's the scoop?"

"Colonel, Sir, a search mission. If we can find the downed plane, and if medical evacuation is needed, we get the mission."

Ron was ecstatic to have a real, as opposed to the boring training flights recently endured, mission. Major Richard Edwards, the 1022nd Operations Officer, was also Rios's training officer. When Rios completed training, he would be the commander.

"Rios, we have a mission in your part of the state. Your sheriff asked the adjutant general for support for a search and rescue operation in Banner and Canyon Counties. Your name may, or not have, been mentioned, but we got the mission

Coldly, Rios demanded, "why wasn't I informed?"

"Sorry, Colonel. I sent Wing to you as soon as I got off the phone," apologized Edwards.

"No, I'm the one that's at fault, not you. If I had been in Caribou, I would have already been in the loop. Let's put this show on the road, or the bird in the air, hi ho silver, and all that."

Other office personnel wondered about the laughter ringing down the hall.

SFC (Sergeant First Class) Jackson Davenport was the crew chief, SP5 (Specialist 5) Ron Wing was the flight medic. Major Richard Edwards and Lieutenant Colonel Rios Rivera completed the flight crew of Cowboy Six.

Jack Davenport gave a half-wave salute to the two officers and reported. "Gentlemen. Full fuel, blades released, tie downs removed, and preliminary pre-flight is complete.

"Thanks, Sarge," Rios said as he gave a full salute back to the crew chief.

The two pilots made a full walk-around inspection. Everyone took assigned places in the UH-60. The checklist was completed, switches moved into correct alignment, and soon Cowboy Six was off the runway and on course for Caribou. Denver Center acknowledged the instrument flight plan and directed, "Lifeguard Cowboy Six cleared to 9,000 as filed. Report altitude changes. Squawk 1320."

"Roger Center," Major Edwards responded.

[Lifeguard is a call-sign prefix signifying a medical priority aircraft. 9,000 is the assigned altitude. Squawk is lexicon for the number to be set on a location transmitter which identifies an aircraft on radar.]

Cowboy 6 landed at Caribou Airfield to refuel and coordinate with Banner County Sheriff's Department. Usually, a local observer would be boarded to help with directions. None were needed. Rios knew the area well.

LIBBY FLATS REVISITED

The Libby Flats board of directors was a mixed bag. Several were computer geniuses. At least two were former spies, although they preferred to be called observers (and some were still spying as they observed the board activities.) Reports were easy to transmit, even from Wyoming. Rich men and women populated the board. Ranchers and realtors provided valuable information to the Libby Flats board.

Wealthy members felt they owned the board since their money kept clandestine operations functioning. Computer-savvy members understood the board goals and assumed they were in control. The rich wanted to be richer and didn't care who led if the board activities put money in their pocket. The ranchers and realtors were figureheads; they didn't live in this realm. Doctor Richmond was the driving force. His goal is to get the miniature 'Cray-type' computer functional, find the right government, and make himself wealthy and powerful as the 'World Spymaster', at least in his mind. This diverse board had common ground and compatible interests. Each member complimented the other.

"Dr. Richmond," Lamar Robinson inquired, "why is the sheriff's department asking us questions?"

"Explain," ordered Dr. Richmond.

"Deputies came and questioned Helen and me, Cookie and Janice. They were asking if Elfonzo was our attorney."

"What did you tell them? Did they mention Libby Flats or the trust?"

"What do you think, Doctor? We refused to talk to them. Libby Flats didn't come up because we cut them off."

"Did the deputies tell you what they were investigating?"

Helen Palmer interrupted, "Elmer is missing. I'm his wife. Or maybe Herman. Cookie is Herman's ex-wife, and Janey is his mother. Elfonzo is Herman's brother and is a lawyer. I told Lamar we should not talk to the deputies."

Lamar added, "and Elmer and I are business partners. If Elmer or Herman, or both, are dead, we may all be suspects. The cops always look for those connections. There is no reason to talk to anyone until we know more."

The board chairman, Dr. Fredrick Richmond, nodded his head in agreement. "Time to have another talk with Bernstein. Kalinda, please have Saul join us."

Saul Bernstein was a graduate of 'Dundalk High'. That was a reference to the military intelligence officer school at Camp Holabird in Baltimore,

Maryland. The intelligence institution was on Dundalk Drive. Saul was a distinguished alumnus. After graduation, Saul served his country as an undercover officer (think spy). His counter-intelligence activities and leadership provided critical information for the United States military, CIA, and FBI activities. When Saul retired from the Army Intelligence Service, he was clandestinely chosen to head the mysterious GSI. Bernstein and his hand-picked operatives knew "almost everything about everything". Saul knew about the Libby Flats tunnel from the Grubb mansion to the vault in the big hole. He was acutely aware of the small but powerful computer, stored inside the vault. The GSI team enjoyed observing the Libby Flats board struggle to gain wealth, keep the laptop and its location secret, and jostle each other to be the 'alpha dog'. In the board's view, 'alpha dog' was not necessarily the leader of the pack, but who could gain most from their 'Tunnel Secret'.

Saul often thought, *"what pompous fools. All this effort to protect their so-called tunnel secret that every government agency, foreign and domestic, knows about."*

Kalinda escorted Bernstein into the conference room and directed Saul to a chair on the side of the conference table.

"Good morning, ladies and gentlemen," said Saul, as he made himself comfortable in the soft conference chair and poured water from the table thermos into his glass. Saul took a sip and leaned back in the comfy chair. "What can I do for the Libby Flats board today?"

"Get the cops off our back," exploded Lamar.

"Where are Herman and Elmer?" asked Helen Palmer.

"Are they dead?" George Smith said quietly.

Dr. Richmond pounded his gavel on the podium. "All of you settle down. Let Mr. Bernstein have the floor. He may have information for us, and some guidance."

The Libby Flats board reacted like well-trained service dogs. The members sat quietly and looked to Saul and Dr. Fredricks attentively. All that was missing was 'good board'.

Saul stood and addressed the board. "Most of you, maybe all of you, except Doctor Richmond, believe I am the head of a security company, a group of rent-a-cops. That is true. GSI does provide your security. That is not all GSI does. We have other clients who have a vested interest in the little box you buried in an underground vault in Caribou.

"You are a despicable spy," observed George Smith. Silence covered the meeting. No one else even made a sound as each imagined the worst - from arrest to being tortured or killed.

Saul let the silence continue. He observed the countenance of each board member and filed the responses in his memory.

"This is not a problem for the board. GSI is here to help you achieve the goal originally envisioned by the Libby Flats Foundation. Doctor correct me if I'm wrong. LFF was able to obtain an extraordinary computer and secure it in a hidden vault at the end of a long tunnel. LFF desires to sell this computer to the highest bidder. Since this computer is both portable and extremely powerful, it is also quite valuable. Is that correct Dr. Richmond?"

Dr. Richmond and the other board members were shaken that an outsider knew this information. Richmond finally nodded in the affirmative and replied, "yes, it is. How did you come to this knowledge?"

"GSI has extensive experience in espionage and observation, or as Mr. Smith said, we are despicable spies. How we obtained what we learned is not germane to my answer. What we do with our knowledge is your primary concern."

Helen Palmer, who was a former spy for the Central Intelligence Agency (CIA), was the first to respond. "What do you want from us, and why should we accommodate any requests you may ask or demand?"

Bernstein sat in his chair, smiled at Helen, and then stared at each board member in turn. Saul chuckled and said, "because you have no choice."

The 'Cray' computer, at one time the most significant and fastest computer in the world, takes enormous, climate-controlled space. These computers are used at the Cheyenne Mountain NORAD (North American Air Defense) system in Colorado Springs, Colorado, and at the space rocket facilities used to put astronauts into (and back) from space. The

Cray-type computer systems take up the area of one or two football fields for the hardware alone. The little computer in Caribou is the size of a small laptop. In that computer, speed is not essential. Memory is king.

<<< >>>

Jim Feltner asked Saul, "what is different about this one. Lots of computers can be programmed for almost anything?"

"Good question, Mr. Feltner. Primarily because the inventor is dead. He left no notes. The only way to analyze his work would be to destroy his innovations. Then no one could utilize the unique capabilities."

"Which are?" Jim replied.

"This program, which GSI has labeled 'Caribou Catch' enables the operator to enter another computer's programs, capture and use them, access all information within the computer memory, block some or all use of the network, and erase everything on the other computer's hard drive."

"So," remarked, Helen Palmer.

Saul calmly replied. "So, whoever has the computer will be able to access every bit of information on every computer in the world. The perfect spy."

"Oh crap," moaned Fredrick Richardson. He then thought to himself, *"we aren't asking nearly enough. This little box is worth multi-billions more than we were asking."*

Others around the table were having similar thoughts and wondering how to improve their status on the board.

Delmar Bushnell voiced what most of the members had considered, "do you know the status of Elmer Palmer and Hernan Story?"

Saul replied, "yes. I do."

Helen shouted. "Well, what is it? Are they dead, or not?"

"Most certainly dead. Two sheriff's departments are looking into both deaths."

<<< >>>

Jerry mounted the big grey horse, shifted his weight back and forth to ensure the saddle was tightly cinched, and led the team out of the corrals at Carl's ranch. Jerry was riding a tall grey gelding and leading two of the packhorses. Jerry had never ridden this horse before, but knew it was a good one. Carl Tafoya had a unique way of naming his horses The better the horse, the shorter the name.

Carl had handed Jerry the reins and commented, "you will enjoy Grey. He has good mountain manners."

Jerry smiled and thought to himself, *"must be a great horse."* Carl names most of his horses with people names. For the outstanding performance horses, he uses the name of the horse's color. Grey or red are great horses. Gruella (a greyish mouse color) or sorrel (red) was used for an above-average horse. Carrie or George would be average. Kalcan,

Kibbles, or other dog food names, were used for mean or hard to ride horses."

"Thanks, Carl, I'll treat him carefully."

Carl and Willy J didn't get along well. Jerry was surprised when Carl put Willy on Blacky.

Carl turned to untie another horse from the hitch rack. He grinned at Jerry and pronounced, "next time maybe, but we are a team right now." Both men laughed heartily.

The riders moved up the ridgeline to a U.S. Forest Service trail into the national forest. The group settled into a routine. It was almost silent, except for the wind through the trees, the creak of saddle leather, and the sounds of horses blowing and snorting as they labored upwards. The whisper of the wind through the trees and the saddle leather rubbing made a peaceful ride up the mountainside. Jerry paused at the crest of a razorback ridge to allow the horses to rest.

"Check saddles and packs," advised Tafoya.

Checks were made. Cinches and pack straps were adjusted and tightened. When everyone was back in the saddle, Jerry instructed, "keep your eyes moving and be attentive. An airplane in the trees or the snow is harder to locate than an elk bedded down."

These men were acutely aware of the difficulty of their task. They nodded and rode out with confidence and hope. As the horsemen moved higher into the mountain area and the slope widened, each moved toward the side of the search area to better observe the terrain they were searching. The trees were not dense yet, but thick enough to limit visibility. Jerry held up his radio and gestured to the mounted riders to listen.

Jerry turned up his volume and opened the squelch (a muting feature of the radio). He could barely hear Charlie 40's transmission.

"Two-Six (Felix Johansen) caught sight of a possible metal or glass reflection. I am turning to look."

"Roger Forty. Cowboy 6 has an rdf (radio direction finder) heading for you. Keep talking. We can only get a reading when you are transmitting," directed Major Edwards.

Rios keyed the intercom in Cowboy Six. "Major, she knows that. Chris did an instrument approach in the snow using a radio station transmitting tower behind the airfield."

"Sorry, didn't know that."

"Cowboy 6 roger, we are approaching that location where the reflection was sighted --------------------." (Chris kept the radio on transmit.)

"I'm used to dealing with civilian searchers." Edwards explained.

"Have you in view, Cowboy Six," Charlie 40 transmitted.

"Copy."

"Cowboy Six will move uphill to your right. You can make turns downhill if necessary."

"Thanks, Six. Let's see what we can find."

This search turned up finding ice and water glare, but no airplane.

ROBERT W. SCHRADER

BUD HAYES SHARES

Carol Ray, County and Prosecuting Attorney Tashana (TG) Gonzono, Court Reporter; and the Honorable James E. Broderick, District Judge; were enjoying a lunch at the Rusty Nail.

Julie Downs, their server asked, "what can I get for you to drink?"

"White wine and ice water, please," replied Carol.

"We have a nice house Chardonnay. Would that be ok?" Julie inquired.

"That would be great.

Tashana ordered, "just ice-water with lemon for me." Julie took a pencil out of her pocket, scribbled the two orders, and looked at Judge Broderick.

"Please give me a Famous Grouse on the rocks and a prime rib sandwich, medium-rare. No court today, a major project efficiently completed, and good company. Nice time to celebrate."

Julie grinned, "and a great location to do that."

Carol and TG both giggled. It was a rare occasion to observe the Honorable James Broderick relax.

"We got it done, Judge. Thanks to a lot of help from the sheriff and Mr. Hayes." Carol was proud of the file moving project.

TG agreed. "The file storage at the Annex is a better system than we had at the courthouse. We can find files quickly."

"You should," said the judge. "I've seen the sheriff's overtime vouchers. I'm glad they did a good job. Enjoy lunch. I'll pay for it myself."

Sergeant Falls dismissed the last detail of box movers. "Let's see if Mr. Hayes has some more ghost stories for us."

David Stephenson, Issac Alzate, and Attilio Bernardo thought that was a good idea. The four deputies made their way to the basement area where Bud Hayes maintained a desk, if not an office.

"Gentlemen. What can I do for you today?"

"Mr. Hayes," began Jack Falls. "We have completed the file moving operation. The four of us were wondering if you had any more stories from the past to impart."

"I always have stories to tell. I am retired with little to do, so there is time as well. Pull up a place to sit."

Mr. Hayes removed his suit coat, carefully hung it up on a wooden hanger, and placed it into the closet. Bud loosened the tie around his neck, unfastened the top button of his sharply pressed shirt, and made himself comfortable in his desk chair. "Let's see, as I recall, we were talking about young people who lived in this old mansion when it was named Mountain Shadows Funeral Home."

"Yes, Sir," Attilio answered, "you called him Master Barton."

"Ah, yes, young Master Barton. He was a live wire as a youngster. He became a skilled embalmer. Later he became a respected medical doctor," recalled Mr. Hayes.

"Issac Alzate objected, "but you were going to tell us about this joint being haunted."

"Issac, this fine mansion was never a joint. And I only said it was haunted in my memories."

"Pay attention, Alzate," suggested Sergeant Falls. "That, in fact, is what Mr. Hayes related to us."

"Sorry. My poor language skills."

That statement made them all laugh heartily.

Mr. Hayes leaned back in his soft chair and again placed his highly polished oxfords on the desktop. "That's ok gentlemen. Bart was sure a ghost named 'Herman' sat on Bart's closet shelf and watched over the youngster. I never saw Herman, so I wouldn't know if this 'joint' is haunted.

Bud's comment brought another chorus of laughter. Mr. Hayes continued, "there was once a newly married couple who occupied the building at night. The husband was an embalmer who responded to requests for removal of human remains from hospitals, homes, traffic accidents, and the like. The wife thought there were ghosts in the building. At least the first time she was left alone at night while her groom went on a removal call."

"Why was that, Mr. Hayes?" Attilio queried.

"When her husband backed the funeral coach out of the garage, he didn't get the garage door shut all the way. That damned door banged in the wind the entire time he was gone. The bride just knew poltergeists were coming after her."

"How did that work out?" Jack Falls drawled.

"After her loving spouse got her calmed down," Bud paused to relight his cigar, take a drag on it, and blew out a perfect smoke ring, "he told her what all deputies should know. Don't worry about dead people, it is the live ones that can hurt you."

"Roger that," said Jack Falls and Dave Stephenson, almost in unison.

"Let me visit the men's, and I will tell you two short stories about young Master Barton during his tenure at Mountain Shadows."

Everyone took a break. Bud re-lit his cigar and stood facing his enraptured audience. Bud was enjoying his role as storyteller. His audience was fascinated by the ancient history recitations.

"I assume you have all seen the small room on the second floor, across from the elevator and stairs."

The four deputies sounded like an echo chamber, "what elevator?"

Bud chuckled and pointed to a pair of side-by-side doors behind the deputies. "Behind those doors is an elevator that gives basement, ground, first and second-floor access. The elevator goes to all floors except the last level where you stored the file boxes."

The facial expressions of the four file box movers, as they each came to realize the elevator would have saved them enormous work, were more than Bud could suppress. He laughed until he had tears in his eyes. Bud used some kleenix to dry his tears and started chuckling again. All four deputies joined in Bud's hilarity.

Mr. Hayes resumed his professorial stance. "As I was about to explain. That little room was called the 'cold room' because it had no fireplace. It did, however, becomes Master Barton's room. Eventually, Master Bart discovered how to lower the crib side. He learned to crawl out of his bed to roam the mansion. One night his parents discovered he was missing from his crib. Bart was found on the first level. He had pulled or pushed a chair next to a casket containing a human body lying in state. That gentleman was dressed in a suit and tie. Bart had a glass of water and used his fingers to flick water on the gentleman's face in the hope that he would awake and play with him."

Issac said, "but no ghost?"

"Depends on what you believe about how ghosts operate," responded Mr. Hayes. "Master Bart's next great display convinced his parents to move out of Mountain Shadows Funeral Home into a home of their own. Ghosts or coincidence, I don't know."

"What did the kid do?" asked Attilio.

Mr. Hayes took a sip from his glass and inquired. "Do you know how a torchier lamp looks. It has a large, round base, a thick post, with a round upward tilted bowl?"

Bud Hayes painted a word picture for his audience. "You are quietly sitting in the funeral chapel. The first hymn has been sung. The minister begins to speak. Then – screaming sounds overhead, and the noise of someone racing up the front stairs to the second floor. Finally, a huge crashing sound, high voices, and a child crying. Silence resumes. The minister continues his sermon. Was all that commotion the sounds of ghosts, or a mischievous child?"

Before any of the deputies could respond, Bud mined someone standing on the base of a tall lamp, rocking back and forth. Then Bud jumped to one side. Mr. Hayes yelled loudly; "kaboom, crash- bang!"

The deputies realized Bart had tilted the ornate lamp back and forth until it, out of Bart's control and fell to the floor over the chapel. Mr. Hayes received a standing ovation from his small audience as they applauded Bud's performance.

"Thanks, Mr. Hayes. I think I understand ghosts much better now," said Attilio.

"Now, you can share my ghosts in your memories," Mr. Hayes told them.

<<< >>>

"Two-Six Delta (Canyon County Dispatch), Three-Three-Sierra-Delta. (Cessna call sign.)"

"Go ahead, Three-Three-Charlie-Forty." Chris realized she had used her aircraft call rather than her tactical call used for the search operation.

"Three-Three at Bingo fuel (enough to fly to the airport with the required reserve)."

Chris had fudged her two call signs into Three-Three. That number was the same in either.

"Roger Three-Three-Charlie-Forty. Advise when back on search."

"Copy Two-Six-Delta." Chris turned east towards Caribou. Bright glare put spots in her eyes.

"Cowboy-Six. Get a fix on me with your rdf. I'm low on fuel, but I may have something in the valley."

"On the way, Forty. Break, Two-six-Delta, Cowboy-Six. See if you can get some of the mounted riders with Cowboy callsigns pointed toward Paint Rock Canyon (a major feature identified on the maps.)"

"Roger Cowboy-Six. What have you got?"

"Me, nothing. From the sound of her voice, Charlie Forty may have spotted something worth examining."

"Two-six Delta, Three-Three-Charlie-Two, my team will cross over the ridge and take a look."

"Copy Two. Break. Charlie-Forty, if you can orbit until Cowboy-Six has a visual, please do. Make fuel your priority."

Chris clicked her microphone twice in acknowledgment.

Her second pass over the area gave Cecil and Felix the correct visual angle through the tall pines.

"I've got a plane in the trees about eighty degrees to the right," exclaimed Cecil Atwell.

Johansen slide to the opposite side of the rear seat to observe the area Cecil had identified. "Yes, that's a plane. Hope it is the one we are searching for."

Chris passed the information to Canyon County dispatch and Rios with two quickly done radio transmissions.

"Forty, Cowboy-Six. I see you, go fuel."

Chris and her team were ecstatic about the find, and equally disappointed. They had discovered the missing plane. They hoped to be present when the plane got inspected, but they wouldn't be there.

Jerry urged the stout grey horse towards the ridge. The grey, and even the two pack horses, seemed to sense Jerry's urgency. Jerry observed the Cessna turn to the east. Soon he could hear the distinctive sound of a

Blackhawk UH-60. He caught a glimpse the helicopter descending below the ridgeline to his front.

"Two-six Charlie-Delta, Cowboy-Six. Aircraft in tree line is red with white trim. No movement has been observed. This plane appears to be the aircraft in question. Cowboy-Six can safely land in a clearing about two hundred yards to the west and deploy flight medic and crew chief."

"Cowboy-Six, Two-Six-Charlie-Delta, proceed. Three-Three-Charlie-Two, did you copy direct?"

"Affirmative. we are about a quarter-mile from the ridge top."

Canyon County dispatch gave the map coordinates Rios had provided from his aircraft navigation radio equipment and directed all search units to that destination.

Everyone on Captain Burkley's team quickly determined the map coordinates were in Banner County. For better or worse, good or bad, this crash was primarily their problem.

Les Bowden was an experienced sheriff. He was also a dedicated law enforcement officer. His horse-mounted team turned toward the crash location and continued to ride and render assistance. Les, Jerry, and the two Cowboy-Six crew members converged at the crash site. None were happy with what they saw. Two adults were strapped into the front seats. They were dead. A faint ray of hope glowed when small footprints leading away from the plane and downhill were discovered by one of Sheriff Bowden's deputies.

Chris had just finished refueling when she heard "small footprints" over the radio. "Cecil, Johansen, we are back on duty. Hurry. The kid must be on foot going down the mountain."

Chris and Cecil Atwood completed a quick pre-flight inspection, ran through the checklist, and were soon back in the air.

Jerry and Doctor Weisberg tightened cinches, mounted their horses and followed the small footprints. "Looks like she is headed to that cabin," observed Bob Weisberg.

"Hope she's there, Doc," replied Jerry.

Burkley and Weisberg discovered a broken door window and signs clothing and food had been taken, but no youngster. The two remounted their horses and followed the small tracks nearly to Caribou. The snow had melted, the mud dried, and the asphalt roads left no traces.

Brynna first sensed she was followed off the mountain as she moved stealthily through the tall trees. She caught glimpses of people on horseback.

"I hope I'm not in too much trouble for breaking into that window and taking stuff — no more snow. I can see a lot of buildings. Hope it's a town. Maybe I can find a place to hide."

It was, indeed, a town. Caribou was a small town, even by Wyoming standards. Caribou was large enough to be the county seat of government for Banner County, with city, county, and even a couple of state facilities like Highway and Game & Fish located in the city.

Brynna found an exciting place to hide. Formerly Mountain Shadows Funeral Home, the stately Grubb mansion sat empty. Brynna found a small window that was not adequately secured. The brave young girl accessed the window and became a resident in the old building.

Brynna also discovered Caribou was large enough to conceal her presence. She was ignored.

Banner County Sheriff's Department and other agencies continued the search. Rios returned from his Army National Guard training. Rivera transitioned into the Jet Ranger, and patiently waited for 'Bill', the county patrol dog, to arrive.

PAPERWORK AND PIZZA

Captain Burkley, Chris Roads, and Rios Rivera, were seated in the Banner County Sheriff's Department conference room. Piles of files cluttered the center of the large table.

"Cheyenne sheriff's office is sending Deputy Brian Taylor, who worked the Story case in Cheyenne. Stands Tall and Doc will join us later. The charts on the wall show what we know, or think we know, about both deaths," Jerry informed his deputies.

<u>ELMER PALMER</u>
<u>Place of Death:</u>	Banner County
<u>Cause of Death:</u>	shot/frozen?
<u>Possible Witness:</u>	Nancy Carmichael
<u>Suspects:</u>	

Helen Palmer - wife
Lamar Robinson - business partner

HERMAN STORY
Place of Death: Laramie County
Cause of Death: Carbon-dioxide?
Witnesses: None discovered
Suspects:
Elfonzo Gutierrez - half-brother
Janice Story - ex-wife
Cochina Paulson - mother

FORENSIC EVIDENCE
Autopsy of each deceased.
Trace evidence at discovery locations.

INTERVIEWS
Nancy Carmichael by C-40/C-20
Helen Palmer by C-40/C-20
Lamar Robinson by C-40/C-20
Janey Story by Cheyenne SO
Cookie Palmer by Cheyenne SO

EXPERT WITNESSES:
Dr. Robert Weinberg, D.O.
Dr. Henry Toshman, M.D.
Dr. Simon Weaver, M.D.

"Grab a file, read it carefully, and make notes. When you finish, and the others arrive, we will try and make sense of what happened. We have two bodies without a known cause of death, no one with a definitive motive for murder, if it was murder. I want these two cases solved one way or another," ordered Captain Burkley.

The files were of three types:
1. The case file with pictures and the initial report.
2. Forensic evidence such as autopsy results, background history of the victim, and lab reports.

3. Witness interviews (see the following sample):

BANNER COUNTY
SHERIFF'S DEPARTMENT
BCSD FORM 33-6
WITNESS INTERVIEW
Case #33-DB-F-001   Status: Open
Victim: Elmer Palmer
SEX; M   RACE: C   HEIGHT: 5'8'
EYES: BR   HAIR: BR   SCARS/TATOOS: NONE
REPORT: # 1   Date: ##'##'####
PERSON INTERVIEWED: Nancy Carmichael
SEX: F   RACE: C   HEIGHT: 5'5"
WEIGHT: 160#   EYE: BR
HAIR: RED   SCARS/TATOOS: NONE
INTERVIEW CONDUCTED BY: CHRISTINA ROADS
DEPARTMENT: BCSD   TITLE: DEPUTY/PILOT
    BADGE #40
INDIVIDUALS PRESENT AT INTERVIEW:
Carmichael, Nancy, Witness.
Rivera, Rios NMI, BCSD, Patrol Supervisor, C-4.
Roads, C. Christina, BCSD, Deputy/Pilot, C-40
[Attach extra sheets BCSD Form #26-6A
to add additional names/information.]
PLACE OF INTERVIEW: BCSD-Caribou, WY.
START/END TIME OF INTERVIEW: 1344-1515
TAPE: Same # as case number
COURT REPORTER: n/a
CASE DISPOSITION: Pending

SUMMARY OF TESTIMONY:
X   Tape
Court Reporter Transcript
X   Officer StatementAffidavit before Notary Public

The witness related she called 911 to report a dead body near Anthem Peak. A BCSD helicopter was dispatched to her location - BCSD Jet Ranger N2033. Pilot C-3, Copilot - n/a, Crew C-1. Witness observed county coroner arrive and remove body. Witness related she gave a statement to C-40. Witness had no additional information. ===END.

FILED: BCSD, Caribou, Wyoming, Records Section.

Chris pointed out the obvious. "What a tedious pile of paper. Someone killed a lot of trees to say nothing."

"True," said Rios, Chris Roads's patrol supervisor and her husband. "Often, the case can be solved if one is patient enough to find the answer. Kind of like turning over rocks to observe rocks to find the information contained underneath the last rock."

Jerry jumped into the conversation. "That's correct, Forty. You want to be a detective, detect."

Somewhat sheepishly, Chris replied, "Yes, Sir," and resumed her reading.

Deputy Taylor joined the group, and after greetings were exchanged, Brian picked up a file and began to peruse the contents. The first sheet of paper in the file was an interview form. There would be many more before Taylor finished reading. The room was as silent as a library reading room overseen by a stern librarian.

Several hours later, Jerry suggested, or commanded, "let's take a break, get something to eat, and then we start brain-storming the information we have gathered to make an investigation model."

Great idea, Jerry. Are you buying dinner?" joked Bob Weisberg, who had just arrived with the chief of the Caribou Police Department, Stands Tall Ferguson. Weisberg was one of the department's reserve deputies. Doctor W. was also a surgeon and Banner County Sheriff's Department chief, (and only) medical officer.

Jerry said, "sure, I'll buy. The vending machines are in the hall."

Jerry's response drew chuckles from everyone.

"How about pizza from Desmond's?" Doc Weisberg asked. "I'll buy the pizza, Dewey (Zolnosky), the proprietor, can deliver and Captain Burkley can pay for sodas from the machines."

Hearty applause ensued. Chris went to the dispatch center to call in the order.

Jerry put the show back on the road. "Ok, what have we got?"

Suggestions and comments were offered. Rios kept track and began writing on the whiteboard.

Assume both deaths are related:
Both deceased worked at Mountain Shadows.
Both deceased were on the Libby Flats board.
Both deceased knew each other.
Alphabet agencies have an interest in each.
Both deceased died mysteriously at the same time.
What is the link?

Assume the deaths were not related:

Insurance money – enough for motive?

Libby Flats stock

Appears to be a family trust.

Several government contracts – more money?

Follow the money trail.

Investigative questions:

More autopsy information.

Why are the feds involved?

Money.

Sex.

Funeral home connection, if any.

"My head's swimming. Lots of information, but no connection," stated Rios.

Deputy Brian Taylor (LCSO) stated, "I agree with Rivera. I've got a long drive back to Cheyenne. I have one major question, maybe two. If we get the answers to them, we solve both cases."

"What are the questions?" asked Chris.

"Simple. Who killed Elmer Palmer and Herman Story? That the first question. The second question is – how were they killed?"

Stands Tall wrapped it up, "heck, let's just arrest everyone and let the judge and the lawyers sort it out." Tall's comment brought hearty laughter from everyone.

"Go back to work everyone," Jerry ordered. "We will finish up and sleep on it. Maybe something will occur to someone."

"Captain," Jerry's secretary called from the doorway, "one of the ag's (Attorney General) legal beagles wants to talk with you. He is on line four."

"Thanks, Sara. I'll take it in my office." On the way out of the conference room, Jerry snagged the last of the pepperoni pizza and wolfed it down on the way to his office. Chewing the last of the pizza, Jerry punched the #4 button, lifted the handset out of the cradle, and asked, "what can I do for you, counselor?"

"Afternoon Captain Burkley. This is Howard Chatham."

"You must be Harley's boy, the 'How' in 'Dewey, Cheatham and How,'" Jerry quipped.

"Young Chatham chuckled. "That was dad's plan, but I escaped. I'm in Cheyenne with the attorney general's office."

"Sorry to hear that. Harley is a defense attorney I admire. We could use more like him in Banner County."

"Thank you, Sir. Pretty nice compliment. I'll let dad know," Howard said respectfully.

"As I said when I answered the phone, what can the sheriff or I do for you today. Plumb happy to help since you apparently aren't calling as a defense attorney. Please call me Jerry."

"Well," Howard began. "The AG needs some assistance," Chatham explained. "We are trying to recover land lease real estate. The leases expired several years ago. Notice was given to the tenants that the leases would not be renewed. The majority took advantage of the state's offer to allow improvements such as cabins and barns to be removed, and moved off the land."

"That sounds pretty fair since improvements become part of the underlying real estate as I recall," remarked Jerry.

"Yes, Sir, that's true. Most of the tenants moved off the land."

"What's the problem. Some of them figured it was their land?"

"Yup. That, and similar arguments. I took them to court and won. The judge granted evictions in all of them. My problem is an armed holdout west of Caribou. Judge Broderick indicated your office was the agency for enforcing his order of eviction."

Jerry dug for more information. "Where is the property and who is the person with the gun?"

"The guy with a .44 magnum is named David Kelly. The land is just about in the middle of the wilderness area thirty miles west of Caribou."

"Can you ride a horse, Howard?" Jerry inquired.

"Of course, doesn't everyone?" Howard responded.

Jerry laughed with a roar. "Not everyone, and most not very well. Do you want to ride along?"

No, Sir, but I will if need be."

"No need, and not necessary. Just thought you might like to see your armed guy arrested. One of my reserve deputies, Willy J., had the pleasure of dealing with Kelly previously. It was at my promotion party when I made captain. I think Willy might enjoy this assignment."

Jerry and Howard exchanged other information. Jerry hung up the phone and shouted, "Sara, would you please ask Willy and Lieutenant Pawlik to see me?"

"Yes, Sir," Sara replied.

Willy Harold poked his head into Jerry's office. "What do you need, Boss?"

Jerry put down his coffee mug and tilted back in his desk chair. "Come on in, have a seat."

Willy sat in one of the comfortable office chairs in front of Captain Burkley's desk.

"Want to go for a long horseback ride in the mountains?"

Jerry took another sip of his coffee. *"Not fair to tease Willie. Of course, it is. Cheryl still has remodeling on the new house to finish,"* Jerry thought to himself.

Willy interrupted Jerry's thoughts. "Sure, where are we going?"

Jerry grinned. "I'm not going. You and Lieutenant Pawlik are the lucky travelers."

"Ok," Willy persisted, "Where are Joe and I going?"

"For a ride in the mountains," Jerry retorted.

Joe Pawlik materialized in Burkley's office and slid into the chair next to Willy.

"Are you crazy. You want us to get on a horse in this weather, ride thirty miles into the forest, take a gun or guns away from somebody, and bring him back here under arrest?"

"You could at least say hello," said Jerry.

"Hello. Is Willy crazy too? It's cold out, and I don't like being shot at by stubborn people. If I shoot, there will be a whole bunch of paperwork for everybody in the system."

"Shucks, Joe, it's only one or two people, not a battalion." (Joe had been in Vietnam too.) "It's getting warmer too. You might enjoy the assignment. Remember the guy at Desmond's when I made captain?"

Willie said, "I do. Sucker was going to shot someone."

"Yeh, and he was dumber than a whole box of rocks. Walks into a pizza joint where almost all the customers were law enforcement, to rob the place," Joe remembered.

"Well, you have a warrant for his arrest. Go serve it and be careful. He is probably more dangerous because he is stupid. As the comedian said, "you can't fix stupid."

"Feds on line two, Captain." Sara Alzate announced.

"Ok," Jerry groaned. "Which alphabet?"

"One of the good ones, Zeke Flores, FBI - Cheyenne."

Jerry picked up the phone handset and greeted the FBI SAIC, "what can I do for you today, Zeke?"

OTHER PILOT'S TOYS

Between the challenges of riding horseback into the mountain wilderness area to arrest and evict an armed trespasser, handling the aftermath of the fire at the Standard Oil station, and regular duties, Jerry was quickly drawn back into a routine. He was making up for missing a month while he accompanied John Burks on his campaign for President of the United States.

"Don't forget. You have a conference call with the Palmer-Story task force and the alphabet federal agencies at 1500," reminded Jerry's secretary, Sara Alzade.

"Thanks, Sara. Please remind me to set up a meeting with those traveling to Oklahoma to watch the election results with the Colonel."

Jerry still used 'Colonel' to mean general or senator for John Burks. Sara wondered if her captain would use Colonel or Mr. President when Burks won the election. She giggled and said, "Cheryl already set up dinner at the Rusty Nail for Betty and Bob, Doc and Bonnie, Willy J., Rios and Chris, and you and Cheryl. You only need to show up. Details are on your desk pad. Big Tom and Edna can't make dinner but will travel with you. The chartered Lear Jet will pick you up at Caribou Field election morning at 0700."

"Is that all, or did you run out of breath, Sara?"

"That's all, Boss." Sara giggled again and left Jerry's office.

The Rusty Nail is a rustic, but extremely comfortable steakhouse and bar; the best restaurant in Banner County. The Nail would be a four-star eating establishment anywhere if you could get the owner, Ed Plant, and his staff to move. Ed is the 'Rusty Nail'.

The exterior is not fancy. Neither is the reception area. But then you enter a large area with a balcony. One wall is stone with a gigantic fireplace in the center Opposite the fire is a long mahogany bar with movable tall chairs. Between bar and fireplace are comfortable sofa-style chairs next to low tables. The atmosphere is relaxed and comfortable. A separate restaurant area compliments the bar section.

Several of the soft chairs had been arranged to accommodate a group of nine. A large file folder was tented in the center. Hand-printed on front and back was 'RESERVED'. The table was saved for Cheryl Burkley. Ed had known Cheryl since she was an infant. Ed also thought highly of Jerry

Burkley. Somehow, neither Cheryl nor Jerry had any trouble making reservations at the Rusty Nail.

The Burkley function tonight was a celebration highly approved of by Ed Plant. The small group about to descend upon his bar had labored upon John Burks's campaign for President of the United States. Tonight, they were making final plans to share election night at the Burks's home in Pauls Valley, Oklahoma.

Two cars with Banner County marking and one private vehicle drove onto the Rusty Nail parking area. The occupants of the three automobiles unloaded and progressed to the Nail on foot. They were greeted by Ed Plant and escorted to the reserved area.

"Good evening, Ed," Cheryl told Plant. "Thanks for all your help tonight."

"My pleasure. Is Burks going to win?"

"Damn right!" Jerry boomed, with similar comments from the others.

Once seated by the fireplace, the men all ordered Famous Grouse on the rocks. Cheryl ordered a 'Colonel.', as did Betty. Bonnie ordered a Chablis. Chris was scheduled to work at 2400 hrs (midnight) and had iced tea. [A 'Colonel' is a martini, made to John Burks's secret recipe.]

Ed Plant and one of his waitresses, Julie Downs, collected everyone's dinner orders. No menus were necessary, all were longtime regulars and knew what they wanted for dinner.

"Thanks, Ed, thanks, Julie," said Jerry.

When the group had ordered and everyone settled down, Jerry rapped a knife against his water glass and addressed the happy bunch. "Ok, guys and girls. We are flying to the Colonel's for election results. Willy has the details."

And Willy did. Ed arrived as Willy finished his briefing and announced, "dinner is ready. Please follow me."

A mass exit occurred as everyone stood and followed Ed to the table.

The Lear was on the ground and had been fueled, serviced, given a complete preflight inspection, and was ready for departure, when the Burkley entourage arrived at Caribou Airfield.

The chatter was about the dinner and today's trip until the Banner County Sheriff's Department pilots, including Chris, (who had just completed her duty shift at 0800), and the two Lear Jet pilots got together.

"Sorry, boys and girl," apologized the senior Lear pilot, "neither of us have instructor ratings in the Lear. You must be type-rated (qualified to fly a Lear Jet) even to sit in the cockpit. We just can't let any of you get any stick time in this plane, even if you could decide which pilot would move up front."

"Makes sense," replied Rios. "The sheriff and Jerry are both pretty picky about who gets up front in our Jet Ranger too."

"You have a Jet Ranger?" the Lear co-pilot inquired. "Nice."

Chris commented, "seems like we all like each other's toys." Her comment brought chuckles and laughter from each pilot.

Jerry closed the discussion. "If you are on this flight, get luggage stored where directed, get on board, strapped in, and let the crew take us to the Colonel's."

"Don't you mean the senator's," asked one of the Lear Jet pilots.

"Well, I mean to the president's when he is elected tonight." Cheers followed Jerry's ad-lib.

"John Burks will always be our 'Colonel'," advised Bob. "I worked for Burks when he was a colonel, a general, and a senator. I still think of him as the 'Colonel'. President may re-arrange my thought process."

The flight to Oklahoma City was short, but long enough for the four Banner County pilots to each spend a little time in the Lear Jet cockpit. Life-long friendships can be built on less.

On the tarmac, Betty watched the moon in the night sky. Later Betty's diary proclaimed:

"The full moon crept above the clouds in the night sky. Cloud fingers made the full moon appear to change its appearance time and again. The clouds gave the impression something, or someone, was holding the moon. Then the moon escaped! Clouds seemed to be blown away from the white orb in the sky by an unseen force.

The moon shined the reflected light of the sun to brighten the earth. Just as the 'Colonel' will be the moon to bring light to our government and reflect the will of 'We the People' in our part of the earth."

John Burks had a house in Pauls Valley. Burks didn't have the space for the crowd that would be present later that election night. Jerrry's group was quartered at a hotel across the street from the Myriad Convention Center where the formal activities began later on election night. Dinner, however, was at the Burks' residence in Pauls Valley. Mrs. Burks was in charge. The Banner County Vietnam veterans felt like they had been transported back in time and into the future simultaneously. Dinner at the Burks' home, wherever geographically located, was a familiar event.

Betty, Bonnie, and Cheryl, were long-time friends of Rose Burks. They flocked to the kitchen to help with dinner. Tom, Edna, and Willy, were entertained by Colonel Burks (everyone, including household staff, called him 'Colonel'). Bob took a familiar position behind the bar and doled out drinks. Doc and Jerry passed appetizers around. Chris floated between the groups.

Chris was amazed to see the kitchen gang, as she mentally labeled Mrs. Burks, Cheryl, Bonnie, and Betty, cut raw beef into chunks and place it uncooked on silver platters. Chris thought to herself, *"Did they all have too many of those good martinis? Should I say something? No. Senator Burks will notice. Or maybe the sheriff or Edna. I don't like rare meat. What can I do that won't cause a fuss?"*

Rios startled Chris out of her thought, induced trance. "Time to eat. Come on. Everything looks delicious."

Chris swallowed twice and hurried after her husband. The dining room table was formally set with china plates and silverware. Each place had a handwritten name designating the seating places.

After all his guests were seated, John Burks lightly taped on his water glass with a silver knife. "Your attention, please. Rose and I are delighted to have you join us on, at least to me, a historic night."

Hands clapped. Jerry, somewhat loudly, commented. "Just another one of the 'old man's missions." Laughter joined the applause.

"Well, I hope this mission is as successful. Rose and I both appreciate all you have done for us."

The Colonel lifted a glass of wine and stood. The veterans quickly rose to their feet, with Big Tom and Willy J. close behind. The ladies took their cue from Mrs. Burks and remained seated. All raised a wine glass for the toast the colonel/general/senator was about to propose.

"To friends, old and new, and their ladies too. May our friendships remain true. Those who wore the Army green, and those who were the glue holding families together tight when their men went off to fight. I make this toast in thanks to you, my friends, and wish you happiness that never ends."

Colonel Burks raised his glass to shoulder level and proclaimed. "Friends forever!" He drank a sip of the wine.

"Here, Here!" responded twelve voices

FONDUE, A NEW TITLE, AND DISCOVERY

Chris wasn't sure what she was going to do with the giant helping of raw steak John Burks piled on her plate after she had carefully selected only two small pieces. She observed her husband use a small two-tined fork to put his first meat cube into the pot of hot oil.Others at the table were involved in the same exercise.

"My worries are over. I can cook my steak in the oil," Chris chuckled as she placed a fork of steak into the round pot of oil.

Betty commented. "the first time I had fondue with the Burks', I thought Mrs. Burks had sipped one too many martinis. This remark brought chuckles that Chris happily joined.

The remainder of the evening went well. The entire group joined a busload of guests going to the convention center. The large television screens displayed a growing lead for Senator Burks, confirmed by a large group of volunteers on a bank of telephones. By the end of the evening, Senator Burks was President of the United States – Elect. After that, no longer was John Burks addressed as 'Colonel'. He would be 'President Burks' for the rest of his life.

Brynna wasn't aware of fondue, a new president, or events outside of the Grubb mansion. The parade of off-duty deputies hauling boxes and people coming and going had ceased. She hadn't seen anyone for several days, not even the nice old gray-haired man. Brynna had moved back into the room across from the elevator on the second floor. She was quite content to continue her exploration of the old building.

The arrival of two men she had never seen before startled her. It was late afternoon and starting to get dark. Never had she observed anyone in the building that late in the day. Brynna crawled into an alcove across from the concrete tunnel she was trying to work up the nerve to explore. The two men went into the space carrying a large box. When they came out, the box was gone. She watched one of the men hang, what appeared to be a key, behind a wooden rafter in the ceiling.

The two visitors used the old elevator to get to the ground floor door. She made sure they were gone and not coming back, then began to make her own plans for the evening.

"I'm going to go to that place where they serve the free dinner. Then I think I will get my flashlight and see what was is really in that tunnel. Maybe I can see what they had in the box."

Brynna sat with some of the kids she had met at the Salvation Army, ate her fill, and carried off some fruit for later.

"Nice of those two guys to leave the elevator on the ground floor, so I don't have to climb up or down after I go through the window."

Brynna took the ancient elevator to the second floor, crossed over to what she thought of as 'her room' and went promptly to sleep. The next morning her exploration continued.

Her expedition was delayed. Carol and Mr. Hayes entered the building mid-morning to finish up the file storage labels. Brynna was in the basement when she heard them enter. The basement steps creaked as Bud Hayes, lugging a sack of supplies, came down the narrow stairwell.

Mr. Hayes banged the sack against the wall several times as he descended the confined passageway to the lower level. Brynna scurried into a large closet in the room at the bottom of the steps. She managed to pull the door shut as Mr. Hayes entered. Bud walked past Brynna's hiding place into the next room. Bud shed his coat and tie, hung them in a cupboard in the next room, and sat at the desk table.

"Good thing I didn't hide over there," thought Brynna. *"I think I have seen this guy before. I hope he doesn't stay long."*

Brynna was not comfortable. The floor was hard and cold. Mr. Hayes heard movement in the next room. Bud put down his nib pen and investigated. Brynna shifted positions. Mr. Hayes thought a rat or other large varmit was making the random noise. Bud pulled open the door. To his surprise, there was not an animal, but a young girl on the floor.

"And who might you be, young lady?" Mr. Hayes inquired.

"Brynna jumped to her feet. "I'm Brynna with two n's," she quickly replied. "Who are you?"

"My name is Hayes, Bud Hayes, and I am here to assist both you, the sheriff's department, and Judge Broderick. What may I do for you?"

Brynna, although wary, trusted the courtly gentleman. "I live here, sort of."

"And why is that?" Bud softly inquired.

"I was in an airplane crash in the mountains with my parents. I got tossed out. Mom and Dad got killed."

"Where was that?"

" Up over there," Brynna explained, pointing towards the high mountains to the west."

"How did you get here?"

"Walked. I crawled in a window here. It was warm. People hand out food at the Salvation Army up the street."

"Come with me Brynna with two n's."

Bud escorted Brynna to the elevator and with extensive experience quickly took them to the second floor and subsequently to the third-floor storage area. This time Deputy Stephenson accosted Brynna's presence. Mr. Hayes ignored the deputy and waived Carol to them.

"What have we here, Mr. Hayes?"

"A stowaway in need of our assistance." Mr. Hayes succinctly explained Brynna's quandary. Carol took Brynna by the hand and called to Deputy Stephenson. "Deputy reach out for Charlie 40. Her presence here ASAP is requested. Deputy Stephenson did not respond directly to the county attorney. He keyed his radio. "SO, Charlie Three-Seven, Charlie Forty to immediately report to the Annex."

"Roger, Charlie Three-Seven."

Bud took Brynna by the hand and led her around the storage floor, much to the disgust of Deputy Stephenson. Although, as he watched, David Stephenson learned. Bud showed Brynna hidden storage areas off the main room she had not yet discovered. "Be careful Brynna with two n's. If you step off the plywood, you might end up next to your room," Bud cautioned his little companion.

"How do you know which room I use?"

"I worked in this building for many years. I have seen your clothes carefully stowed away."

"Oh."

"Mr. Hayes, Chris Roads is here," called Carol.

Bud and Brynna joined Carol and the lady deputy.

"Mr. Hayes. Would you introduce your friend to Deputy Roads?"

Bud did so, with great formality. Carol then explained to Brynna that she would be temporarily placed in foster care until other custodial arrangements could be arranged.

"No way," Chris interrupted. "Rios and I will take care of this brave young lady. She is not going to one of your homes for castoffs."

"Will your husband agree?" Carol asked with a smile on her face.

"Of course. Rios just flew to Florida to bring us an addition to the family. One more will be perfect."

"Are you adopting, and I don't know about it?" Carol's face showed amazement.

"No adoption, except a dog. I didn't know either." Chris chuckled. "When Rios told me he had been promoted and was going to be the K-9 department commander, he told me his patrol dog, Bill, would be living with us. I think Brynna with two n's, and Bill with a badge, will be a good fit."

"You have a dog?" Brynna exclaimed, "and you want me to live with you. Can I?"

"I believe that can be arranged." Carol chuckled.

Mr. Hayes inquired, "may I be of assistance?"

"How about all these nice people. The nicest is a cop. Will she arrest me? Probably not, if she is going to take me to her home," thought Brynna. She turned to Bud Hays and said in a shaky voice, "thank you so much. I'm glad you found me, and I trusted you."

"Me too, my little Ghost."

RIOS GAINS TWO

Rios Rivera was working with Bill when his sheriff's department cell phone vibrated on his belt. *"I hate that."*

"Hello."

The caller was the Banner County and Prosecuting Attorney, Carol Ray.

"Hi, Carol. What can I do for you?"

"Be nice to Chris when she calls. She just took in that lost kid."

"The one from the mountain? She has been found? Is she all right?"

"Brynna is fine. If Chris has her way, she will be living with you."

"Great. A new dog and a new kid. I hope she is housebroke."

"Is the dog?"

"Should be. Bill is about 18-20 in people years."

"Brynna is ten going on forty. You and the other Forty (a reference to Chris's badge number and nickname) will have a house full."

"Ha. I can hardly wait to meet her."

"Her name is Brynna with two n's. You two may even get along."

"Thanks for the heads up. I've got to go. The dog folk are here.

Rios, Lisa, and Bill, boarded Banner County's Cessna. Bill seemed to be used to airplanes. The trusty patrol dog curled into a ball and promptly went to sleep. Lisa and Rios talked all the way to Caribou.

Rios buckled Bill into his new BCSO kevlar vest with a badge marked K-9 on each side. Bill promptly assumed the heel position next to his handler, sat, and awaited the next command. Putting on the vest meant Bill was on the job and going to work.

"Forty (Deputy Carlita Christina Camino Roads) and Brynna (with two n's) entered the Banner County Sheriff's Department conference room. Chris took Brynna's hand and led her to Rios and the black Lab. "Nice to have you home. Looks like we have introductions to make."

"Yes, we do. You know a lot about Bill, but Bill and I know little about the young lady with you.

Brynna went to Rios, held out her hand, and announced, "I'm Brynna with two n's, and I'm staying at your house. My room there is nicer than the one I had in that old building. The one at your house has a bed."

Still in sit position, Bill managed to inch himself towards Brynna.

"Can I pet Bill?"

"I don't know. Are you able to do that? Rios teased.

After a moment's hesitation, the light came on, and Brynna asked, "May I pet Bill?"

"Yes, you may. And thank you for asking."

Bill and Brynna quickly bonded. Bill was secure with Brynna. The big dog rolled onto his back, legs in the air, and moaned like a cat purrs as Brynna rubbed his tummy.

"There is someone else you both have to meet." Captain Rivera gently tugged Bill's lease. Bill jumped to his feet, assumed the heel position, and sat. Rios unhooked the leather lease and commanded, "Bill, find Lisa."

Bill sprang forward and ran through the open door. Bill immediately returned, followed by Lisa Sloan.

"Ladies, this is Lisa. She made it possible for Bill to be part of our family. Pretty unique, a pretty foster daughter and another law enforcement partner join the Rivera family. Lisa will be staying with us too, but only for a week."

"But a great week," said Lisa. "I get to see my Bill in his new role as a police dog, meet y'all, and help set up the sheriff's K-9 division. I also got to meet Brynna."

Rios cautioned Lisa, "Bill is not a police dog. Bill is a sheriff's patrol dog."

"I stand humbly corrected," Lisa said, laughing with the others.

Forty said, "Lisa, Brynna, would you like to go for pizza.

"Yes."

"Yeah."

"Me too," said Rios.

"Good," exclaimed Chris. "Sheriff Tom expects us at Desmond's at 1800. Bill and Brynna can ride with Rios. Please come with me, Lisa."

At Desmond's, Bill did what was expected of a good service dog and went under the table to lay down. Old habits are hard to change. Most patrol dogs remain in the car, unless they are working. Neither Rios nor Bill had that training. In this case, a lack of training turned out to be fortuitous.

Desmond's seems to be a magnet for dumb bandits, or this bandit was extremely stupid. David Kelly once tried to use a gun to rob Desmond's. The pizza joint owner liked cops. The night of Kelly's previous visit there were in attendance almost all the Banner County Sheriff's Department. Kelly pulled his gun and got a full pitcher of iced tea over his head and arrested for his effort.

Tonight, Kelly tried again. Handgun in his hand, he demanded Dewey Zolnoske give him the money in the cash register. Dewey looked at Rios, who nudged Bill and commanded, "gun".

Bill shot out from under the table, hit Davis mid-body, knocking the dummy down. The gun skated across the linoleum floor to rest next to Tom Flannigan's chair. The sheriff retrieved the stray weapon and turned to watch Bill guarding Kelly with quiet growls each time his prisoner moved. Rios gave the command for Bill to "leave it." Bill went back to his place under the table. Rios patted Bill and said, "good dog."

The sheriff cuffed Kelly. Soon a patrol car transported Kelly back to his previous jail cell.

"Quite a dog my wife encouraged me to get," pronounced Big Tom, followed by a big bite of Desmond's pizza.

"Brynna slid under the table and hugged Bill. "Bill is such a good dog. I'm sure happy we are friends."

EXPLORATION

Sometimes working dogs get to play. Louis (dog trainer and reserve deputy) recommended equal play and work. That became the norm for Delta and Bill. Brynna thought that was fantastic - she had two dogs to play with, and each on a different schedule. More playtime for her.

"Can you drop Brynna and me at the Annex on your way to the SO (sheriff's office)?" Chris asked Rios at breakfast. "I told TG and Carol I would help with the rest of the labels."

"Sure. Can you take Bill with you? I will be in a meeting all day. I am sure Brynna and Bill can find better things to do than having Bill lay next to me."

"That's nice," thought Brynna. *"Bill and I can go see what's at the end of the dark tunnel. I have a flashlight in my old room, and we can use that elevator to go down to the basement. And, I will have Bill to keep me safe."*

Brynna had a mission for Bill and herself. "I am going to take Bill out for playtime," Brynna informed Chris.

"Ok, sweetie, have fun. Don't go out of the yard."

"We won't," Brynna assured.

The little girl and the black Lab bounded down the stairs and made loud noises getting on the elevator. Chris and Carol surmised Brynna was going to the ground floor - Brynna went on to the basement.

"Ok, Buddy." Brynna praised Bill. The dog wagged his tail happily. "Let's see what we can find."

The tunnel was dark and long (no lights and being underground created the darkness. The tunnel was long because it crossed the street in front of the Grubb mansion and went half-way across the lot on the opposite side of the road.)

Brynna's flashlight helped. Finally, she and Bill found the end of the tunnel. They came to a dead-end.

Brynna thought, *"there has to be another door. Otherwise you those guys wouldn't need to leave a key."*

Brynna shined her light around - nothing in front or to the sides. Nothing on the floor. Then, she noticed a step stool and looked up. A padlock hung from the ceiling, attached to what appeared to be a small door. Brynna petted Bill, and said, "I think there is a small ladder in the outside building. Let's go see."

Brynna and Bill were outside in transit to the barn when Carol came out to check on them.

"How are you guys doing?"

"Really good," said Brynna. Bill just ran around and wagged his tail - this was his first playtime of the morning.

Carol smiled, "have fun."

Brynna giggled. After Carol left, she got the ladder and took Bill back to the long shaft. Eventually, the ladder was in place beneath the door, the lock was unfastened, and Brynna gained access. Brynna pushed up on the door, which caused her ladder to wobble under her. *"That's kind of scary."* She used one hand on the opening to balance and pushed the door up. Suddenly it swung up. *"Must be spring-loaded."* The door caught on something and remained locked in the upright position. A bright light came on and illuminated a small room. Along one side was a pull-down ladder like you see in the movies on fire escapes in big cities. This ladder was slanted at an angle. When Brynna pulled on a rope handle at the bottom, the contraption slid down and became a regular set of stairs.

Bill bounded up the stairs and circled the small room. Brynna climbed down her ladder and walked up the stairs into the brightly lit room.

"Wow. Sure, a lot of effort for a little room with a cardboard box in the middle. Oh, a laptop on the box. Wonder if it has any games?"

Resting on the cardboard box was a small laptop computer. A lengthy cord was plugged into the only electrical outlet.

"I wonder if it works?"

Brynna opened the little laptop and watched the screen take life. Large black letters pronounced, "CONNECTED TO," and then began scrolling government type shields and insignia. Brynna saw some that looked like those she had seen on TV, like FBI, CIA, and U.S. Army. Many were strange and foreign appearing. The panorama ceased.

The screen showed, "QUERY? _____"

"Query? Am I supposed to ask the computer questions? Let's see."

Brynna knew how to type. She put in all kind of questions; how high is the moon? where have all the flowers gone? how do mice get out of their maze? After listing 15-20 more crazy questions, the inquisitive little girl poked the return button on the keyboard.

No questions were answered. The shields scrolled across the screen and "Query? _____" appeared.

Brynna hit the keyboard keys at random. Same results.

"No games, darn."

[The QUERY? _____ was a programed response by the computer. An operator could type in a code to have responses displayed to the screen. The computer program did continue to process the information the young girl had typed. Much was forwarded to intelligence agencies worldwide. After all, that was what this little computer was designed to facilitate. Informally called 'Translator' by operators of the many supercomputers attached. Translation was only one feature. No other computer had all the available data. 'Translator' did. Brynna's random letters, numbers and symbols were treated as reality.

<<< >>>

Cray computers, the massive, fastest, most sophisticated computers in the world take space. The small laptop in the tunnel vault was unique. The chip wired next to the hard drive gave access to smart computers like Cray and the experimental one south of Cheyenne, Wyoming. Satellites fed and received information with a code The antenna for this little computer was embedded in the concrete box placed at the end of the tunnel several years before. The laptop was a recent addition.

Brynna had silently watched some men who were not cops bring the box into the basement tunnel. She did not trust them either. Brynna had a cozy cave in the east side where she watched without being observed. Now she knew about the computer, but not what it could do.

When she went to leave, Brynna tried to shut down the small computer, but was not able to get any response other than "QUERY? _____ "

Brynna tried to retract the stairs - same luck. The stairs stayed in place. With the stairs down, she couldn't close and lock the door either.

"Come, Bill. We must go find Captain Rivera and see if he can help us put things back in place. He will know what to do."

MOBILE RIVERINE FORCE ASSOCIATION

The Mobile Riverine Force Association is a group of Army and Navy veterans who served with the Mekong Delta Mobile Riverine Force (originally named Mekong Delta Mobile Assault Force) in Vietnam. The Mobile Riverine Force (used a reinforced brigade of the 9th Infantry Division and associated combat support units like D Company, 9th Medical Battalion, based on Navy ships. Navy assault groups were used for tactical mobility (military talk for how the Army traveled to perform their part of the mission). In the MRF, the Army lived on Navy ships, went to work on Navy boats (or sometimes Army helicopters), slogged in the mud like other grunts, and returned to the boats. A great joint effort by Navy and Army to bring the war to the enemy.

The Mobile Riverine Force Association (MRFA) was created in 1992. The association has a reunion every two years. Although President Burks was never assigned to the Mobile Riverine Force (MRF), he conducted several operations with, or using, MRF personnel. As Colonel Burks (and later as General Burks) John R. Burks was an honorary member of the association. The association leaders made a request for President Burks to be the keynote speaker at the next reunion. The invitation was accepted, sparking excitement in Caribou, Wyoming. Several members of the sheriff's department had served with the MRF. Others had been involved in Mobile Riverine Force operations.

Sheriff Tom Flannigan, Undersheriff Marvin Glen, Joe Chambers (Detention Captain), Rios Rivera (K-9 Division Captain), and Jerry Burkley (Patrol Captain), were seated casually around the conference table. Only two pieces of a large double pepperoni remained in the Desmond's Pizza box. Chuck Williams brought information from dispatch.

"What have you got, Chuck?" Big Tom asked.

"Strange night. Other than the usual, all the cell towers shut down. Dispatch had a lot of radio interference. Then about ten minutes ago cell and radio returned to normal operation."

"What caused that?" Marvin inquired.

"No idea, yet," replied Chuck. "If I find out, I will let you know."

Chuck serendipitously snagged the last two slices of pizza and strolled back to dispatch.

"That reminds me," Rios injected. "Our new dog and his play buddy, Brynna, discovered a tunnel under the Annex. The tunnel led to a small room above the end of the tunnel. Inside the room is a small computer that seems to do nothing. Maybe it caused the interference, maybe not. The timing was about right."

"How did you find out? asked Tom.

"Brynna told me after she couldn't retract the ladder and close the door. She's inquisitive, but a terrific kid."

"Well, stay on it." The sheriff ordered.

"Yes, Sir, will do."

The discussion reminded Jerry of a tunnel/computer discussion in Germany but didn't quite make the connection. The sheriff changed the subject to personnel.

"Jerry, I assume we are looking at five or six officers wanting vacation time to go to the MRFA reunion since President Burks is speaking."

"Yes, Sir, three regulars; Rios, Forty, and me. Doc and Bob are reserve deputies. Forty will be going as a wife. All the rest of the wives are going. I flew missions for the MRF so I am also going."

"Ok, we can manage," commented Tom. "Last item, retirements and re-organization. Marv retires at the end of the month. Jerry, you are the new undersheriff. Win the election, and you will be the new sheriff in Wyoming. Pick your new patrol captain."

<<< >>>

The Banner County group drove to Denver. No one had devised a plan to use the department's aircraft. All the deputies felt naked without their sidearms. Airport security at Denver International Airport was, well, it was airport security.

Arrival for the reunion was better. A local volunteer provided a ride to the hotel. The rooms were ready for occupancy. Soon the Wyoming vets were seated in the bar area. MRFA members were everywhere, and conversations began. Most contacts started with "when were you there? what did you do? what unit?

Tonight, the MRFA members were part of a large group. Tomorrow they would group with their units.The reunion featured speakers, breakout rooms, tours to local attractions, and a large area where members could visit with old friends and new. They shared stories began, "back in the day". Photos, slides, videos, and conversations between friends followed.

The Wyoming group had special status. These were the guys who got the wounded out of harm's way, and either fixed them or sent them on the road to recovery. They were welcome almost everywhere. The secret service was everywhere. Their job was to make the area safe for the president.

The president took the stage. I mean, he took it. John Burks talked. The veterans listening felt Burks was speaking directly to each. He was! They had all shared the same or similar combat experiences. No applause was necessary, but could not be stopped. After the speech, President Burks, much to the chagrin of his secret service security detail, remained in the room to shake hands and talk with the brave veterans. The security detail finally managed to herd the president to his car. Burks signaled Jerry to join him.

"Nice speech, Mr. President."

"Thanks, Jerry. I really enjoyed being at the reunion. I am pleased you and your bunch could be here with me."

"Our pleasure, Sir. "

"I understand that you are now the undersheriff. Are you going to run for sheriff?"

"That's what Sheriff Tom and my wife say. I filed before we left to attend the reunion. I will start campaigning when I get back to Caribou."

"Outstanding. How is the lost girl doing?"

Jerry was astounded the president would remember about Brynna. "Rios and Chris have her. She seems to be adjusting well. She trusted Rios enough to tell him about a tunnel and a small computer she discovered in the old Grubb mansion, that we call the Annex."

Jerry's information caught the president's attention. "Tell me more about the computer, please."

"Well," Jerry paused to collect his thoughts. "The computer is small, it was plugged into the only electrical outlet, with no other visible connections. It may, or may not, function. The screen scrolls identity crests or insignia with the same request."

"What is the request?" asked President Burks.

"Query?" responded Jerry.

"Is that from the computer or a question from you?" asked President Burks.

"Sorry, Sir. That is the computer's response to any entry."

"What else?"

"All cells went down, and most radio communications incurred interference. It reminded me of a conversation I had with Captain Fordham in Germany. "

"What was that?" the president inquired.

"Captain Fordham told me about radio transmissions his team intercepted in Germany about a tunnel and a computer believed to be someplace in Wyoming."

"The following, Mr. Burkley (referring to Jerry's military rank, and changing the conversation to an official exchange of information) is to be considered "Top Secret-Presidential."

"Yes, Sir."

The president shared the details of a briefing he received soon after his election as President of the United States. The presentation, which wasn't brief, concerned a missing, small, but potent computer. I will have Captain Fordham contact you soon."

EDNA MAKES SOME SUGGESTIONS

Captain Fordham on line three Jerry," announced Jenny Abbote.

"Thanks. I'll take it in my office."

"Good morning, Sir. What can I do for you?"

Colonel Pruter called and informed me President Burks requested I brief you on 'Translator.' This briefing will be classified Top Secret-Presidential. Can you travel to someplace where there is a secure phone?"

"Yes, Sir, we have one in our dispatch center. The number is listed in the FEMA classified directory."

"I have it," said Captain Fordham, "ten minutes." Jerry's phone went dead.

Jerry went to the soundproof cubicle in dispatch and waited for the phone to buzz.

Two hours later, Jerry had information to connect many facets of the two murder investigations:

1. The American in Donaueschingen, Germany, is named Cecil Winegar. He is a CIA Agent.

2. The little computer was stolen from a U.S. Military Security Agency. Since Banner County Sheriff has possession of the equipment, it was no longer classed as missing.

3. GIS is a clandestine U.S. agency involved in the computer search effort.

4. Corrupt government agents are suspected in the theft of the computer.

5. The laptop had been swiped from the original thieves.

"That's all I have right now, Jerry. I enjoyed working with you in Germany."

"Me too, Captain. Thanks for the update."

"No problem. Just doing what Colonel Pruter said the president desired."

Jerry was laughing as he disconnected the encrypted phone. He had received similar calls from Colonel Don Pruter. Jerry was sitting at his desk when the humor wore off. Sara walked into Jerry's office and said, "Colonel Pruter is on line one."

Jerry moaned, picked up the handset and pushed button one. "Howdy, Don. I assume you have more for me."

"Of course, the Old Man said to use the information as needed. The president wants you to get the computer to Fort Carson G-2 (post intelligence officer) as quickly as you can."

"Yes, Sir, I'll send it on the Jet Ranger today."

"Great," exclaimed Colonel Pruter. "The president said to be sure and read tomorrow's paper." Don hung up.

Jerry called to his secretary. "Jenny, please have dispatch radio Rios, Bob Schrader, and two of the reserve deputies working today. Have them report to me."

"Roger that, " said Jenny Abbote.

Jerry left his office, walked to the sheriff's office, closed the door, and sat.

Tom looked up from his paperwork. "What's on your mind, Jerry?

"I just got a classified briefing from that Navy intelligence officer I worked with in Germany. The briefing followed a conversation I had with the president. Right after, I got a call from Colonel Pruter. All three calls involved the little computer we recovered from the Annex tunnel. The briefing wasn't brief. Two hours in the secure cubicle is not fun. Anyway, I'm sending the computer to Fort Carson on the Jet Ranger."

"Ok," Tom acknowledged, "and?"

"I'm sending Rivera and Schrader to pilot, and two reserves to guard the computer until we can return it to the military."

"And?" urged the sheriff.

227

"I think our two dead bodies, the one you and I recovered, and the one in Cheyenne, may be tied to the computer and where it was found. I would like to have the county attorney and maybe some, or all, of the alphabet agencies, get the information in a joint meeting. The president said I could use the classified information if necessary."

Tom picked up the report he had been reading. "Alright, I can wait. Set it up."

Jerry left Big Tom's office. Andy Shepherd shouted from dispatch, "call on five for you, Captain Burkley."

"Thanks."

Once again picking up the phone from the cradle, Jerry said, "Jerry Burkley. What can I do for you?"

"Hi, Jerry, Doctor T, boy, do I have some interesting autopsy results for you."

"Do we have another victim I don't know about?"

"Sorry. I mean about the Palmer autopsy."

"What's up, Doc? I apologize, I just wanted an excuse to say that."

Doctor T and Jerry both laughed.

"Ok, what are you talking about?" asked Jerry.

"My wife and I went to Cheyenne yesterday. While my wife was trying to melt my credit cards, I wandered into one of those new fitness centers."

"So?" Jerry countered, "was an autopsy being done at the fitness place?"

"No. The exercise place had the usual array of electric and mechanical machines, but no autopsy. The management was promoting a new technique called Cryogenic Therapy for pain relief. Similar to the ice bath used by professional athletes."

"What does that have to do with autopsy results, Hank?"

Jerry put his phone on speaker, swung his boots onto the desktop, and leaned back in his chair, thinking this conversation might take some time.

Hank continued, "it put the Palmer puzzle together. I now think Palmer may have been shot while he was in one of those nitrogen gadgets, left to freeze, and the body dumped where the hiker discovered it."

Jerry pulled his feet off the desk and swung the office chair around. He knocked his coffee cup over. "Then we have a murder, make that two. Thanks, Doc. Got to talk to the county attorney."

Captain Burkley tossed a towel over the spilled coffee and went to Sheriff Tom's office.

"What's up, Jerry?"

"That's what I just said to the county coroner. I think my 'what's up, Doc?' was funnier than your 'what's up, Jerry?'." At least at the time. Palmer is definitely a murder, and I think we may be able to tie both crimes to the Libby Flats bunch."

"Good work, Captain. Are we ready for a referral to the prosecutor?"

"Yes, we have evidence the ownership of both the Grubb mansion and the adjacent property where the tunnel is located, was owned by the Libby Flats Foundation. Both deceased worked for Mountain Shadows during the period the tunnel was constructed. We have sufficient probable cause to get some search warrants issued."

Big Tom commanded, "so, do it."

Captain Burkley did.

<<< >>>

CARIBOU DISPATCH
Caribou, Wyoming
[Front Page]

PRESIDENT BURKS ENDORSES
JERRY BURKLEY FOR SHERIFF

In what this paper believes is a unique and historical event, a sitting President of the United States of America has formally endorsed a candidate for local office. Endorsements are frequently made for national candidates and sometimes candidates at the state level.

President Burks not only gave Jerry Burkley a glowing recommendation but purchased with his own money (not the government's money and not just a press release) a full-page advertisement in this paper stating his reasons for his message to 'Elect Jerry Burkley Banner County Sheriff'.

[SEE AD ON PAGE B-1]

NEW SHERIFF IN WYOMING

The first-page editorial and the president's personal advertisement endorsing Burkley for Sheriff was just the beginning. A series of events coincided to make history in Banner County.

The first event was unexpected. For several months, a former deputy sheriff vigorously campaigned for the elected office of sheriff. The day following the Burks endorsement, the former deputy withdrew from the election and announced his support for Jerry Burkley. Jerry was unopposed for sheriff.

The evening of the announcement, Big Tom and Edna were enjoying a quiet evening at their home just outside of Caribou, Wyoming. Edna commented, "You know, Jerry, the son we never had, is in effect your replacement as sheriff."

"True," reflected Tom, as he tamped his pipe and lit a stick match. He waved the match over the pipe bowl and took two deep drags on the old pipe. The smell of pipe tobacco filled the living room. "No one else can file for election, and it is doubtful anyone could get enough write-in votes to win. So, yes, I believe Jerry Burkley will be the new sheriff of Banner County."

"Well, I was thinking," suggested Edna, "You could use up some of your accrued leave time, and we could, maybe, go someplace for a real vacation. Jerry knows the job and has a good staff."

Tom thought to himself, *"Oh, Oh. I wonder what she has planned."* Tom knew his wife well. It was one of the reasons the sheriff's department had a new K-9 division.

"Maybe," Tom mumbled, knowing he was taking a trip someplace.

The second event was the appointment of Jerry R. Burkley as acting sheriff of Banner County while Sheriff Tom and Edna took a cruise to Alaska.

Tom entered Jerry's office, closed the door, and sat.

Jerry looked up from his paperwork. "Is this deja vue in reverse. This seems like a replay of yesterday."

Big Tom chuckled, "yup, in a way. Edna and I were talking last night. Seems I am going to drive to Seattle and get on a boat to Alaska. That means you will be acting sheriff until after the election."

Jerry was dumbfounded. "I'm happy for you and Edna. You deserve a vacation, but it seems too soon for me to take over."

"Well, it isn't, you have been doing a lot on your own already, and I will be here for a few more weeks. That should be enough time for us to get the pending cases handled. You get the new problems." Sheriff Tom dictated.

""OK, Boss, what's first?"

"Set up the meeting and follow up investigations on the dead bodies, make the necessary arrests, and get the bad guys in jail," quipped Tom.

"Yes, Sir,"responded Jerry. Captain Burkley directed his secretary to set up a meeting with the alphabet agencies. Captain Burkley called Carol Ray.

"Morning, Captain. Have something for me, or is this a pleasure call?" Carol chirped into the phone.

"Both. Do you want business or pleasure first?"

Carol grinned, "pleasure first, always."

"Ok, it may be business too. Yours, not mine." Jerry blurted. "Rios and Chris want to adopt Brynna."

"How nice. What a lucky girl."

"Yep! And what two lucky deputies." Jerry added.

"That sounds like pleasure, not business," Carol pointed out.

"Rios, Forty, and Brynna with two n's, want you to be their attorney for the adoption."

"I don't see any conflict. I would be happy to join that family as one. What a great assignment."

Jerry was relieved and happy with Carol's answer. He was afraid she might say no. "Fantastic. I will tell them. Now, for business. We may have the Libby Flats bunch, or some anyway, for the two murders and computer espionage."

"Why do you think that?" Carol was intrigued, "this would be an exceptional case."

"I have some Top Secret-Presidential information, our own department investigations, and an educated guess. Our working premise is one or both of the deceased, and/or other Libby Flats board members stole the computer, hid it until it turned up in the Annex tunnel, and were trying to sell it to the highest bidder."

"Sounds weak to me," challenged the prosecuting attorney.

"Do you think it may be enough for search warrants for the board members, their homes, and the Libby Flats holdings?"

Carol scribbled some notes on her legal pad and told Jerry, "I will come over to your dispatch center and listen to the rest in that little room."

Jerry grinned. He was on his way.

The following day, Sheriff Tom Flannigan (BCSD), Zeke Flores (FBI, SAIC-Cheyenne), Howard Chatham (Wyoming Attorney General's Office), Saul Bernstein (GSI and also covert CIA), Captain Burkley (BCSD), Sheriff Willis Van Devanter (Timber County SD), Sheriff Les Bowden (Canyon County SD), and General Phillip Wynott (DCI), were seated in the sheriff's department conference room.

Jerry rapped three times on the table and spoke to those seated around him. "I have deputies posted around this meeting. Captain Rivera and his officers are authorized to use deadly force to enforce security. This meeting will include a classified portion, labeled Top Secret-Presidential. Dissemination of this information is not authorized. In other words, keep it in here, and within this group for now."

General Wynott objected, "that information should not be released, or any classified information for that matter, until all present have proper clearances."

Jerry commanded, "President Burks authorized me to use this material as I deem necessary. If you have objections, you may leave if you wish."

"The Deputy Chief of Intelligence considered the offer for a moment, and replied, "I believe I will stay."

"Thank you for your cooperation. I have some preliminary matters. The first is that I am the acting sheriff of Banner County as of 0800 today. Second, I have deputies, in cooperation with other sheriff's departments in Wyoming, executing search warrants on suspects in two murders and the computer theft/spy conspiracy. Those cases belong to Banner County Sheriff's Department."

Sheriff Burkley's last announcement brought several shouts and objections. Jerry grinned and ordered, "you are free to leave too. This meeting was set up as a courtesy to you and your agencies. I hope to have your cooperation and assistance, if possible, but Banner County has the case. Our prosecutor and I can do it without your assistance if we have too."

Everyone elected to remain for the briefing, although each was trying to figure out a means of taking over the case.

"Sheriff," Lieutenant Chuck Williams called from the conference room doorway, "Captain Pawlik is on the radio. He needs to talk with you on a landline (telephone)."

I'll be right there." Jerry turned the briefing over to Tom.

When acting Sheriff Burkley returned, he announced, "One of the search warrants turned up a .45 caliber automatic pistol. Preliminary ballistics show this weapon may have been used to kill Palmer. The County Attorney, Carol Ray, has obtained several arrest warrants from Judge Broderick, which are being served as I speak. This meeting is adjourned. After the subjects are questioned and I have more information, I will let you know the results."

Howls of protest rang out. Jerry left the room and went to his office.

SECRETS OF THE TUNNEL

CARIBOU DISPATCH
(headlines)

-SEVEN ARRESTED
-ORPHAN ADOPTED
-NEW SHERIFF ELECTED
-FEDS ASSUME JURISDICTION IN
-MURDER/ESPIONAGECASE
-DIRECTORS CONVICTED

Big Tom Flannigan and his wife, Edna were seated before the fireplace in the Rusty Nail bar. Tom asked his waitress, Julie Downs, for a glass of Chardonnay wine for Edna, and a Grouse on the rocks for himself. For the first time in many years, Tom was off duty, and tonight was an exceptional occasion. For former Sheriff Tom Flannigan, it was his retirement party. For Jerry Burkley, it was a celebration of his election as sheriff. A third celebration was for three special people - Rios Rivera, Chris Roads, and their newly adopted daughter, Brynna (with two n's, as Brynna would quickly announce). Tonight, the Rusty Nail was the place to be for celebrating the old, the new, and the future.

Edna and Big Tom arrived early to relax and then to greet everyone as they arrived. For a short time, it seemed that everyone was named 'Sheriff', as everyone still called Tom, Sheriff Flannigan. Jerry arrived, and he too was addressed as Sheriff. Visiting sheriffs from across the State of Wyoming and were addressed as sheriff.

'Sheriff, Sheriff' was almost a litany as they greeted each other. The crowd grew and expanded from the bar into the dining area and eventually into the outdoor patio, with a steady stream of people finding Tom, Jerry, and the new family, to congratulate and exchange greetings, as well as several who made frequent trips to the bar.

Jerry Burkley became the Master of Ceremonies only because no one else was so inclined. Applause began when Jerry stepped onto the dance floor stage and picked up the microphone. Jerry tapped the mike to ensure it was working and said, "Howdy."

Shouts of "Hey sheriff" and "Sheriff Jerry," were loud.

"Nice to see everyone here. Sheriff Tom. Edna. Please stand." When the applause and noise died down, Jerry commented, "a lot of years, a great sheriff, and the power behind the throne." Loud laughter broke out amongst the assembled crowd, most of whom were law enforcement.

"This year," announced Jerry, "we have had a few failures. We didn't get to prosecute some bad people (a reference to the success of the federal agencies and the United States Attorney for the District of Wyoming, in having venue for the Banner County investigation and arrests transferred to the U.S. District Court, in the Libby Flats case), but your efforts made it possible to obtain convictions. We had some victories as well. We had a hard time finding a lost little girl, but when we did, she and our new K-9, gave us the clues to solve three major cases. Brynna also found herself a new family with your favorite Undersheriff, Rios Rivera, and his wife, a deputy sheriff, now a sergeant we usually call 'Forty'." Much more laughter followed this comment.

"To all of you who were involved in any way; Tom's career in law enforcement or Brynna's new family, thank you."

When the applause stopped, someone shouted, "what about you, sheriff?"

"Shucks, I didn't have to do anything to get elected. I had all of you." More laughs.

Jerry was about to step down from the stage when Willy J stopped him. "Chuck has a phone patch from dispatch that you may want to put next to the microphone."

Jerry took the offered handheld radio, keyed the transmitter, and said, "Charlie One."

The radio crackled, and a strong voice announced, "Jerry, this is John Burks. Can everyone hear me? Over."

"Yes, Mr. President. They can. Over."

Captain Williams skillfully worked the phone patch and the radios on both ends, so the conversation and the president's speech to the assembled crowd flowed smoothly.

When it was time to end, Jerry said, "thank you, Sir. Your words were appreciated by everyone here, especially me."

"My pleasure, sheriff. By the way, Mr. Burkley, you may get a call from Don." Then the president terminated the call by stating, "clear."

Chuck closed the patch, which was only getting a dial tone.

"What was the Mr. Burkley and expect a call from Don all about?" inquired Cheryl.

"I'm afraid to guess, but I think it may mean, "HERE WE GO AGAIN!"

PREVIEW

READ THE BEGINNING OF ANOTHER ONE OF JERRY'S STORIES

RAVEN AND THE JUDGES

Corrupt politicians are causing problems for Sheriff Jerry Burkley. An evil man is called 'Raven' for a reason. There is nothing kind about this man. Find out what is kind. Another ''Who Done It' Wyoming style.

b

RAVEN AND THE JUDGES

An older term for a flock of Ravens is an 'Unkindness'. This word correctly better describes corrupt public officials, businesses, and many politicians. The Raven is a stately, large black bird, impressive to watch. Ravens are associated with Apollo, the God of Prophecy. Maybe the ability to see into the future is why the Raven is a symbol of bad luck.

d

KILL SHOT

Greg Monte saddled his horse, tightened the cinch, put his left foot into the stirrup, and mounted the large bay horse. Monte rode the bay up the trail into the national forest. His ride was short.

The shooter lay in the edge of the timber, the 30-06 rifle loaded, the high-power telescope focused on the trail. Greg Monte approached. The shooter smiled, focused the crosshairs on Gregg's head and caressed the trigger. The sound of the rifle rang across the valley. The second sound, a large caliber bullet striking bone, was not loud but carried the distinctive impact thump to the hidden sniper. Monte fell from the bay, his head exploding like dropped watermelon. The horse ran back the way he had come.

<<< >>>

"Nine-one-one, what is your emergency?" asked Jenny Abbote, the on-duty Banner County Sheriff's Department dispatcher.

"Two of my hunters found a dead body." advised the caller.

Jenny inquired, "who is calling, and where is the body located?"

"This is Homer Rinehart. I run Banner Hunting. The body is next to forest trail 647 about three miles from Anthem Peak. Looks like he was shot."

<<< >>>

Kelly Moore had the nickname, Raven. Kelly merited the description. A Raven depicts crooks, especially elected crooks. Nothing is more corrupt than a crooked judge. The Honorable Kelly Moore, District Judge, 30th Judicial District for Luther County, Wyoming, had been on the bench for ten years. Judge Moore was retained in his first election and surprisingly again in is second. Moore discovered means to line his pocket soon after. The Honorable Judge Moore had three more years before the voters could vote him out. Chances of the general public doing that were slim. It took a majority of those voting on to reject a judge. The system was loaded in favor of keeping judges. Many who even voted in an election, and too few exercised their Constitutional privileges, did not vote on judges. Those voters did not understand that failure to vote on that issue was a vote for retaining the judge.

Three years ago, soon after the judge celebrated winning his retention election, a woman connected with Moore in a bar. The Honorable Kelly Moore had consumed three vodkas on the rocks in the belief no one would smell the alcohol on his breath.

Wendy Schultz sat next to the inebriated judge, turned on her sexy charm, and touching Kelly's hand with her fingers, informed Moore, "hi, I'm Wendy. What are you drinking? That looks good."

Judge Moore thought, "*Wendy looks good too.*"

"Just vodka on the rocks, with an onion. May I get you one?"

"Oh, yes. Please," simpered Wendy, batting her eyes and smiling brightly at Kelly Moore, as she patted his hand up and down.

One drink led to several. The 'Honorable' drank his right down. Kelly didn't notice Wendy wasn't keeping up. Moore was pleased when Wendy went to his room with him. The sex was right; it was the best the judge could remember ever receiving. Future meetings with Wendy were arranged by Judge Moore.

"I just have to see you again," Kelly told Wendy Schultz.

"Me too," exclaimed the young woman. Where do you live?"

"I'm in Lusk, Wyoming, but could meet you in Casper or Gillette."

Arrangements were made. Kelly Moore told Wendy many things. He neglected to provide his marital status. The Honorable Kelly Moore was married. Wendy Schultz knew. That helped Wendy and her cohorts use the Honorable for their purposes.

Sheriff," exclaimed an excited Marie Bondurant. Marci was Sheriff Jerry Burkley's newest dispatcher.

"What can I do for you, Marci?" Jerry asked.

"Sir, you have a phone call from the president, The President of the United States!" Marci was jumping up and down in excitement, her hands moving like a band conductor.

"Calm down Marci. Is it the president, or Mrs. Jones?" Jerry calmly inquired.

"Yes, Sir."

"Which one, Marci?"

Marci looked bewildered, like a deer caught in the headlights. She blinked twice, then was back on track. "Sorry, Sheriff. The caller is the president's secretary, Mrs. Jones. She asked for you and said to tell you President Burks was calling."

"Thank you, Marci. Please close the door on your way out."

Marci was disappointed she wouldn't get to hear the president, but said, "yes, Sir," shut the door and skipped back into the dispatch center.

Jerry sat at his desk, picked up the phone from the cradle, and said, "Jerry Burkley, how may I help you."

Mrs. Jones replied, "Good morning, Jerry. Hang on. I'll put him on."

Almost immediately, the voice of John R. Burks came on the phone. "Good morning, Jerry. How is Wyoming's new sheriff?"

"Doing quite well, Sir. We caught Witters, the guy who kidnapped Cheryl, got the Army's computer back to them, assisted the United States Attorney for the District of Wyoming to obtain six convictions for grand

h

larceny and three murders, and not only found a missing orphan but got her adopted by two of my deputies. "

"Pretty nice record for a new sheriff," praised the president

"Thank you, Sir. It was the people who work here, not the new sheriff," Jerry replied.

Jerry and President Burks were old friends. They talked at length about family and friends. Finally, President Burks brought up the reason for his call to Sheriff Burkley.

"I need some assistance, sheriff."

"Sheriff, not Mister?" Jerry inquired, referring to Jerry's Warrant Officer military title John Burks generally used to alert Jerry to an army mission assignment.

Raven was the nickname given to the corrupt politician while still in school. No one liked the sucker. Most detested everything Raven said or did. Despite his popularity, or lack thereof, Raven managed to become an elected public official, and not only be re-elected, but to move upward in the political chain. While Raven was charming votes and getting enough to be chosen, no one liked or trusted the man named Raven.

"Get that new general on the phone for me, Honey," Raven commanded his secretary. For a change, Raven was not sexist. The secretary's name is Honey Blomquist.

"The new Space Command general or the Missile one?"

"The Space guy first, then the other one when I hang up."

"Ok, Boss."

Corruption grows and expands like a prairie wildfire

KEEP UP WITH BOB

Bob Schrader has a website and a FaceBook page. You can access either to keep up with Bob and Sheriff Jerry Burkley.

WEBSITE:

www.robertwschraderauthor.com

FACEBOOK:

http://m.burkleyseries.facebook.com

E-MAIL:

burkleybooks@gmail.com

TUNNEL SECRETS CHARACTERS

BANNER COUNTY SHERIFF'S DEPARTMENT
SWORN PERSONNEL

SHERIFF: Jerry Robert Burkley

ADVISER TO SHERIFF: Thomas Flannigan

UNDERSHERIFF/K-9 DIVISION COMMANDER: Rios Rivera

PATROL COMMANDER: Joseph Pawlik

DETENTION COMMANDER: Joe Chambers

DISPATCH SUPERVISOR: Charles D.Williams

NAME	RANK	BADGE
Jerry R. Burkley	Sheriff/Pilot	C-1
Thomas(BigTom) Flannigan	Adviser to Sheriff	S-1
Rios Rivera	Undersheriff/Pilot	C-2
	K-9Division Commander	K-9
Joseph Pawlik	Patrol Commander Captain	C-4
Joe Chambers	Detention Commander Captain	H-1
Charles D. Williams	Dispatch Supervisor	D-1

	Captain	
Mick Nicholson	Day Shift Supervisor Lieutenant	C-17
Casey Brown	Swing Shift Supervisor Lieutenant	C-12
Sid Koslowski	Midnight Supervisor Lieutenant	C-3
Fred Carlson	Day Shift Sergeant	C-10
Carlita Camino (Chris Roads)	Swing Shift Sergeant Pilot	C-40
Jack Falls	Midnight Shift Sergeant	C-15
Don Fredericks	Day Shift Lead Deputy	C-11
Felix Johanson	Swing Shift Lead Deputy	C-21
Ira Wheaton	Mids Shift Lead Deputy	C-31
David Stephenson	Patrol Deputy	C-37
Dan Taylor	Patrol Deputy	C-38
Ivan Morton	Patrol Deputy	C-36
Terry Brewster	Patrol Deputy	C-26

BANNER COUNTY SHERIFF'S DEPARTMENT STAFF

Name	*Occupation/Job*	Miscellaneous
Molly Cook	Chief Dispatcher D-1	Molly's Service Dog becomes first BCSD K-9
Andy Shephard	Dispatcher D-7	BCSD
Sara Alzate	Dispatcher/Secretary D-2	BCSD

Jenny Abbote	Dispatcher/Secretary D-6	BCSD

BANNER COUNTY SHERIFF'S DEPARTMENT RESERVE DEPUTIES

CHIEF OF RESERVE: ILT Robert W. Schrader, C-20

ASSISTANT CHIEF OF RESERVE: 2LT Willie J. Harold, R-2

CHIEF MEDICAL OFFICER: Robert A. Weisberg, D.O., R-4

Name	Rank	Badge
Robert W. Schrader (pilot)	1LT	R-1/C-20
Willie J. Harold	2LT	R-2
Cecil Atwell	SERGEANT	R-3
Robert A.Weisberg	DOCTOR	R-4
David Ballard	DEPUTY	R-5
Tracy Reed	DEPUTY	R-6
Donald Davidson	DEPUTY	R-7
Steve Rasmussen	DEPUTY	R-8
Louis Robinson	DEPUTY	R-9
Eric Gonzolez	DEPUTY	R-10
Vernon Zolnoski	DEPUTY	R-11
Izac Alzate	DEPUTY	R-12
Hank Toshman	DEPUTY	R-13//P-1
Attilio Bernardo	DEPUTY	R-14

OTHER LAW ENFORCEMENT

Name	Department	Miscellaneous
Stands Tall Ferguson	Chief of Police- Caribou, Wyoming	Old Man Ferguson's Son
Zeke Flores	FBI	SAIC Cheyenne
Saul Bernstein	Global Security, Inc.	CIA undercover
Willis Van Devanter	Timber County Sheriff's Department	Sheriff
Walter Gist	Timber County Sheriff's Department	Undersheriff
Carson Shoemacher	Wyoming CID	Director
Les Bowden	Canyon County Sheriff's Department	Sheriff
Howard Chatham	Wyoming Attorney General Officer	Civil Division Harley Chatham's son
Brian Taylor	Laramie County Sheriff's Deputy	Cheyenne, Wyoming
Jake Bowman	County	Undersheriff

LIBBY FLATS BOARD OF DIRECTORS
Dr. Fredrick Richmond, President

1. George Smith 2. Herman Story
3. Kalinda Canton   4. James Feltner
5. Helen Palmer 6. Delmar Bushmill.
7.Elmer Palmer   8. Lamar Robinson

EVERYONE ELSE

Colonel John R. Burks	POTUS
Rose Burks	FLOTUS
Cheryl Hefner Burkley	Jerry's wife
Betty Schrader	Bob's wife
Bonnie Weisberg	Dr. W's wife
Brynna (with 2 N's)	Orphan at large
Bud Hayes	Ghost story teller
Barry Coleson	Justice of the Peace
Velma Cookson	Drunk driver
Edna Flannigan	Big Tom's wife
Dewey Zolnoski	Desmond's Pizza
David Kelley	Stupid robber
Carl Tafoya	Hunting Outfitter
Julie Downs	Waitress-Rusty Nail
Tom 'Cash' McCall	Car dealer
Simon Weaver	Pathologist
Julius Binger	Navy Intelligence
Michael Reed	Navy Intelligence
CAPT Darwin Wynott	Director, NSA
Jackson Davenport	Helicopter crew chief
Ronald Wing	Army medic
Tammy Fitzgerald	Molly's daughter
Velma Shepherd	Singer-Molly's funeral
Liza Sloan	Dog breeder
Cecil Winegar	The American (CIA)
Herr Rudolph Gulde	Anwalt (Lawyer)
COL Donald Pruter	President's Liaison
Nancy Carmichael	Nurse – witness
Carol Ray	County Attorney
James F. Broderick	District Judge
Tashana Gonzolo	Court Reporter
Ed Plant	Rusty Nail owner
CAPT Sid Fordham	Navy Intelligence
1LT Trevor Smith	Hospital MSC officer
Jill Bascom	Wolf Hotel manager
Herr Max & Gretchen	Sur Zonne Hotel
Mac McGonigal	Embalming Professor
Master Barton Larimore	Funeral Home kid
COL Swartz	Student Commander